Life
After
Chronic Trauma

Jeanne Callahan

PAGE PUBLISHING
Conneaut Lake, PA

First originally published by Page Publishing 2023

ISBN 979-8-88960-108-1 (pbk)
ISBN 979-8-88960-112-8 (digital)

Printed in the United States of America

Introduction

My letter about Ma:

No one can argue that Mom's ninety-three years here on earth wasn't interesting if you listened like I had to throughout my lifetime. But one must have to hear with many different types of ears to understand her spin on the subject and what was and wasn't reality to find that kernel of truth. However, I can with confidence state that she did leave a mark and her effect on the future for so many people. It is hard to acknowledge she is gone, because for me, her voice can resound in my psyche. Yet at her life's end, she had a stroke and heart attack, and she lost the ability to speak. This had no effect on her ability to communicate her displeasure which means she did without missing a beat. She lost her battle finally silencing her, but I still find it excruciatingly hard work to silence her as I always have.

Over what my wife refers to as "my eons," I used to say something to professionals and friends alike, and yet I was deafened by my own utterances. It wasn't until I was talking to my wife and then my sister-in-law, Susan, how warped this thinking was but here goes; *we were three kids raised as only children.*

I am more than aware that this is my viewpoint. I continue to experience that this is how I felt and, at times, still feel. I have two older brothers whom I spent little time with. My time was spent exclusively with my mother, at her hand, infused with her thoughts and the world viewed through her eyes. I was enmeshed right from the womb until now. From the age of five years, I spent my life trying to shake it and her handling of me. It was too much to live up to and the expectations changed too often. I never knew who she wanted me to be, when and what aspect of her life she needed me to fill for her. This, unfortunately, led my life for the first sixty-one years of living a life from her mindset, not so much my own. My own was and is there, but my internal overlord was her—Mom, Jean Caudle—making those judgments I took to heart as any child of a parent would.

But by the time they're adults, one would be more involved in their own world view, their own feelings. Mine were coated in the gooeyness of my mother's misunderstandings of the world, hence when I was in therapy by the time I was twenty-six, on my own of course, there was no family help offered because it was not convenient to find out what it was I needed. Not even for me as I was not important enough to be considered. I was in my late twenties when my parents finally divorced, and I wondered about these clear memories. What a lovely childhood reminiscence to ask your fifty-three-year-old mother about, and she said she didn't remember, and she insisted it probably didn't happen. She would cut it off and not entertain anything that would mean she had to discuss herself in a reflective way that was too scary or painful. She'd out and out lie if required. As you get older, you question yourself, and so I actually asked my dad when he finally returned to the family after about twenty years, but he had Alzheimer's. (I am sure he had Korsakoff, which is a form of dementia but is due to alcohol/drug abuse.)

Dad did say things that were sensible from time to time, which are referred to as a moment of clarity. He said he didn't know about the memories. He said, "I do know she (Mom) would be her usual pushy self and say things like I wasn't doing enough or being enough." This sounded like Mom to me. Then he said, "She'd wonder why I threw 'shit' at her. Your mom is a piece of work, you know. But you two are thick as thieves. Hated both of you sometimes." I walked away with the normal feelings of the warm and fuzzies as a person would. By then I was in my thirties, and I moved out to Scranton, Pennsylvania, with a girlfriend. It was about two hundred miles away and was the best and worst thing I could have done.

Chapter 1

I was born on September 28, 1959 in a small corner of Philadelphia called Torresdale. I am the youngest of three children and the only daughter. My brothers are only two and four years older than I am, yet you'd think they were unable to acknowledge us as siblings.

For her reason only known to her, she kept me separated from the boys, and I've always said Mom raised me as one of her siblings rather than a daughter. But there was so much that surrounded her behaviors which have taken me a lifetime to sort out yet knowing why doesn't quell the damages done. Through no fault of my own, I have had to do work on the undoing of all the emotional land mines left behind.

My father was not a large man; he was typical for the times, and he became more and more mentally unstable as time progressed. My childhood was riddled with him having to go in and out of mental hospitals for his breaks with reality. Mom would almost always say, "Your father was fine until you were born, Jeanne Marie." As most kids would've done, I took that to heart and believed without reality that my father's behaviors were my fault somehow. This was only the beginning of the chronic trauma of my childhood.

Dad suffered ungodly from BPD, bipolar type 1. It wasn't declared for many years when he became the prolific alcoholic where he became enraged. He'd keep us up all night with his listening to Jim Croce, wherein I cannot listen to his music. And it could be difficult when it is blaring in your earholes while one is gassing up the car or is in a store that is blaring *muzac* or elevator music sneaks it in. He'd be up all night raging and drinking, pass out for a bit, and then often he'd go to work. Yes, he'd get up and go to work, which means he was still shot in the ass most mornings.

He and my mother would fight and argue about anything. Not money, not what the kids were doing, but about them and throwing personal insults at each other. It was often quite physical and emotionally disturbing to hear as a child until I left home at sixteen. Dad was a scraper type of fighter, and I knew that because of him actually hitting and fighting a neighbor when I was a child under five. For some reason, I recall that day my mother received a rollaway dishwasher for the house. A male neighbor made a comment toward my mother that Dad didn't like. The night before he was calling my mother a fat bitch—and all she cared about were her kids (his kids too)—this person made an advance toward my mother. My father beat the clothes off this guy. Seriously, the man's shirt fell off from the physicality of the fight. No police were involved, just a fight. I don't know if Mom did anything to provoke this gentleman's interaction, but she didn't seem to mind seeing men fighting over her.

Mom didn't get she was a PITA, or a royal pushy pain in the ass. She wanted what she wanted and that was that. She'd manipulate and argue until she got what she wanted, which included my father's functioning as a parent and as a man working where he did. Dad was a banking attorney and considered one of the best in his field during his time. He did a great deal, but prior to this, he was a history teacher, wherein he went to school at night to get his jurisprudence. He obviously was able to do that and carry his family all at the same time. This all from a man whose parents were forensically diagnosed with severe personality disorders, a.k.a. DID, or they called it split personality disorder and schizoaffective. Dad came from a severely messed up family, and he didn't hide it. My grandfather and grandmother fought constantly, and I never understood why they had separate bedrooms until later on in life. But they were always fighting, and my grandmother went by two names. Dee Dee and Edith. Her name was Edith, and she was one person when Edith was around and my grandmother when she was Dee Dee. When I was two, on a little toddler's bed with buttons on the headboard. I was settling into bedtime, playing God. I'd push a button and say it was going to rain or tomorrow would be sunny. Dee Dee must have heard me and came in. She told me never to marry a Black person because I'd have zebra-striped children. Mom heard her and got her out of my bedroom. Then Mom said that what my grandmother said wasn't real, whatever you hear. Mom wasn't openly racist (she was bigoted against a lot of people).

Then there was the last time I was babysat by Dee Dee. I was about four years old and was put to bed in my grandmother's room, where she would sleep with me or I with her. That night she got into the bed, and I asked her how old she was. She wasn't best pleased with me for asking that and said, "Over twenty-one." Then she got into the bed with me and reached under her pillow, and there she had a paring knife. I was not too scared because Mom used one of those all the time. Then she said, "Never sleep with your husband. Always have a knife under your pillow just in case." I told my mother. They found someone else to babysit us who was a parent of a family friend.

These two—Pop Pop and Dee Dee—raised my dad and his sister and his sisters' eldest child, Glen. My grandparents wouldn't let Dad do as he wanted, which was to play football, basketball, swim, or even have a pet. Dogs to them were dirty. Then my grandfather said to his son, my father, that he wished he were a greased pig instead of his son, at least he'd be worth something. Then the poor guy had to hide athletic clothes to play with his friends or at school. One day someone took his street clothes, and Dad got the shit kicked out of him for that when he got home. My grandmother was so angry that her little boy was in harm's way.

Dad went on to college and competed in multiple sports. I had a picture of him doing an Iron Cross on the rings once. I was always impressed with his abilities when he was young. He'd even take me to his basketball games at the YMCA when I was a toddler. I can remember him picking me up to put me up on a bleacher, and I sat watching him, falling in love with my daddy as a little girl would. It didn't match the man I would see at home though. However, even then I knew what my father's relationship with his parents was like. He hated them, yet he did deal with them the best he could, which was minimal as time progressed.

Mom, on the other hand, had to fight tooth and nail just to finish high school. My parents were raised during the Depression, but they had completely different experiences. My father's parents had work. My grandmother worked for the government, and my grandfather worked real estate somehow. That's what my parents said. Mom's parents were different. My maternal grandmother, whose name was Lourinda, wanted to be an entertainer. She could sing well, as did my mother. Mom's family was very musical and entertainment oriented. My grandfather, Herman, was a truck driver and was born and raised in and out of orphanages while growing up. Mom said his mother was the neighborhood "mattress back," and he had it hard as a kid, and only wanted him around when he was old enough to work, like eight to nine years old. He was a very handsome man, and my grandmother was a beauty too. They just were different. My grandfather worked throughout the Depression, but he was a prolific gambler, losing the rent money more than once. Mom said they often would have to move for that reason. So by the time Mom was going to high school, they felt their eldest should go to work and quit school. They did and she had to support them too. She worked while going to high school in order to finish. Mom trained as a secretary, and her mother took every penny of income except for money she needed for transportation or the old PTC. Mom learned not to tell them about her raises. There was an incident to show that this went further than just finishing school but how narcissistic her mother was too and had jealous tendencies toward her five girls (four survived to adulthood). My mother wanted a ring she saw. Mom showed her this ruby ring and gushed on how much she wanted the ring. It was my mother's birthstone. My grandmother, Lourinda, bought it knowing Mom had wanted it deeply for herself. It wasn't even her birthstone. Yes, she bought it and showed Mom that she bought it for herself and not Mom. That story landed on me by the time I was about six or seven years old.

I remember as a little toddler being at a 5 & 10 store. There was music playing in the background, then my grandmother, who was shopping with us, started to sing. I mean, sing loudly along with the tune "There's No Business Like Show Business," and all I could do was stare at her, yet I was enthralled by her singing and how loud she could sing. But Mom always stated that her childhood was excellent and without the severity of what her husband had been through. Her life was a fairy tale if you let her tell it. Her mother was a unique mouthy woman who sang well, and "Daddy" was perfect and easygoing for the "girls." These families produced our parents. As my eldest brother stated, my father was the most narcissistic person ever until he met our mother, where he met his match. Then these two married and had three kids who needed attention. Life wasn't about them uniquely or alone. They had to think about others who were theirs, and that would interfere with their narcissistic personalities.

I have so many memories from very early childhood; it is amazing. For example, when I was eight to nine months old, during an incident that I confirmed with my mother, I clearly recall a bedroom with ballerinas on my walls. I recall a man was what I thought was ironing something in my room. He'd offer me these humongous cookies the size of your head, which were just gingersnaps. Of course that was my infant perspective. Mom explained he was hanging wallpaper in the room. I was in my crib looking out on him, and he talked to me throughout the time he was there. I still can see the ballerinas. Whomever said that we do not lay down memory tracks from that age is just plain wrong.

Other memories include me getting my legs out of my old-fashioned playpen jail. I got to the sounds I was hearing near the stairs, and what did I see? Handbags being thrown and my parents in a huge fight, yelling and screaming and throwing things. Great examples! I got scared then Dad hit Mom, then the fight was over. I was between ten and eleven months old when I witnessed my first domestic abuse with my parents. For us, it was the norm and thought that was what life was like everywhere. I didn't know any different. I just knew he was scary but so was Mom when she yelled and cried. So I believed that the man kept the woman in line, so to speak.

My mother told me then that her mother said that it was her life, and she had to deal with it. Mom explained that her mother was jealous that we as a family were well-off and she wasn't. Mom also said that her mother told her when she had Tim, her mother stated she wasn't a built-in babysitter, and I never had my Grandmother and Pop Pop babysit us either.

My brothers had their own experience of them, differing from mine, but we experienced each other's childhood too. I heard and saw a lot, watching from the sidelines and not being involved in the boys' lives that much. Instead my mother tried to keep me close to her vest, that other one that she could talk to, and this reared its ugly head again in my life when I returned from abroad after many years.

My parents went back and forth like this throughout their thirty-two-year marriage, which ended in divorce. The fighting was incredibly violent and, at times, very scary to the point where to this day I struggle to sleep at night past a few hours. Mom insisted that I take her side and be her confidant, which was unfair for a child under the age of adulthood.

Living in this household was not for the faint of heart. I was ten years old when my parents and our neighbors across the street during a drunken night at our house decided without my consent to go to South America, which was their home country, and take me too. What one may consider a great opportunity was for me, nothing less than terrifying. The decision my parents made was for me to travel and stay with the family through the summer. I had no relationship with their kids. In fact, I didn't like being around them because of how boisterously loud they'd be. We were around the same ages, but there was no connected relationship, and I had to live with them in a different country for the summer. Plus, they'd speak in Spanish when they didn't want you to understand them. Now I'd be in a country where I didn't speak the language.

Another aspect of my fear was that I had gotten my period when I was nine years old, hence, I'd be in a foreign country wearing belts of the time for pads. They were uncomfortable and messy. I felt a great deal of pain and would have to take pain medication to counter it. Sometimes I couldn't get up or walk with the pain. I didn't want it to be known that I had my period, and I didn't want to be considered even weirder than I already was. I struggled with having a period at such a young age because of an incident that transpired not long before having to go to Ecuador.

I was so embarrassed one day when we were playing touch football outside of our house. I had to wear a belt because tampons were not what my mother wore, and I had to do as my mother said then. I had this on, wherein the pad's tie to the belt fell out of my pants and made it look like I had a tail. Playing a game with the kids, one of the boys grabbed it and made extreme fun of me. I wanted to go into a hole and disappear. I worried about this when I was told I was going on this trip without my parents. I was ten, a child who was shy and enmeshed with her mother. What a horrible thing to do, but I went.

Mom paid a high price for this because she didn't have her confidant there with her. I didn't know why she sent me knowing how she leaned on me. I got there and everything I was concerned about was made real, which included more than I would ever have expected that were both positive and negative.

I was having my period when the water was only on for so many hours a day. A few earthquakes and not getting along with the girls while we were there. I had to share my time with them, and I spent most of my time waiting for a call home. I wanted to go home the entire time I was there. This was a poor country, and the one thing I learned was to be happy to be an American with all we had. I learned how lucky we were compared to most people. But I was lonely, scared, and struggled to get through the time we were there. I got home and didn't want to ever travel again. Well, that didn't happen. Little did I know, it was a precursor to the travels I'd have as an adult.

The time I spent in South America as a young child of ten was terrifying at times. The family was a very nice family, to be honest, but the daughters were "cliquish," and they were sisters—something I've never experienced. The oldest was a boy, and I got along better with him than the girls. There was another girl that came, who was loosely described as their son's girlfriend. He was about fourteen then as was she.

We all flew out of New York one late spring day as we were transitioning to summer. Our first stop was Miami, and then we flew to Panama. That was my first experience of meeting People of Color speaking with British accents. I was so enamored by this that I found myself staring at the police officer at the airport when he said something to me in English with an incredible British accent. He said something to me akin to "What's wrong? Are you okay?" I was fine. I was sadly, typically, socially inept and didn't know how to hide my shock or surprise when something unexpected took place for me.

So I stared and he said, "What is wrong?"

And all I could stutter was "Are you British?"

He responded with "Uh, yeah, and what of it?"

I said to him directly that he was the first Black man I ever met speaking with a British accent.

He responded with a huge laughing smile and said, "Yeah, how many Black people have you met? How do you know that we all aren't British?"

And we laughed.

I said, "I don't know," and said that "Anything can be true I guess!"

He said that I was more right than I even realized and then he helped direct us to where we needed to go, which was a freaking prop plane.

Yes, a prop plane. You know, the ones with four engines roaring in your psyche for as long as you are in that plane!

We all trundled into the small prop plane, all six of us. It was ungodly loud inside, but we were to be on it for a short jaunt from Panama to Quito Ecuador. The flight was pummeled by a torrential storm with thunder and, yes, lightning. We were constantly buffeted and blasted by strong winds, knocking the plane around like a slippery wet fish flopping on a wet deck. We'd drop suddenly and back up again, rolling us from side to side. Stuff, just people's belongings slid around, and it was terrifying. I remember thinking that I didn't know how I ended up there and why I was going to this place and felt so painfully alone and scared. No, I was terrified because I had no one to go to, no one I could trust, and know I could get any comfort from, and it didn't change the entire time I was there.

We stayed at one of the children's grandfather's homes, which was considered "middle class" as he was a physician. He lived there alone with a few dogs and some women that ran his home. They were three South American Indian women, and they were referred to as the grandfather's maids.

One of the women was "slow" as I was told. She would be given jobs like folding napkins. She was also the one who told us when the water was on for us to use. For a few hours a day, we had running water in the house, but we had to fill the tubs up in the house and buckets, and that was what we had for the day. This also ran the toilet. When you used the toilet when the water was off, you'd grab a bucket, fill it with water, and pour it into the cistern of the toilet, so it could be flushed. I was a little girl from the Philadelphia and surrounding area. This was more than foreign. It was scary, but it is what we had to do to have water. That included washing clothes, cooking, cleaning and for the toilet, and personal hygiene.

Also, the house was directly across the street from the police station, which doubled as a jail. The jail had police and a wall around it, and it was about six feet high. Atop the wall was broken glass, jagged pieces of rock, and some rebar sticking up. If we looked out the window upstairs, we could see over the wall, which was rare to see anyone outside except for cops.

The home we stayed in also had a wall surrounding it as well as most homes. Donned across the top of that wall was broken glass too. The grandfather's dogs were inside a chain-link fence that ran in the backyard during the day, but at night, they were let out. One was a male German shepherd named Julia. That's because the grandfather loved that name and really didn't care that it was considered a female name. I remember finding that so very funny as a ten-year-old. The surrounding area was mountainous and beautiful, green and lush in some areas. Of course you are on the equator so temperatures were, in my opinion, weird.

It could be beautiful in the morning when you came outside where the "maids" hung the laundry. Cooking was done in another outbuilding with a fully stocked kitchen. As the day progresses, it warms until it warms up into the nineties. I remember one night we all went to a circus. In the afternoon we had all been outside and got a lot of sun. I got a bit of a burn and so did Fred. We found the cold extremely uncomfortable and strange, especially as we were peeling.

The weather was generally nice, and we were there during our summer. The kids in Quito were in school. Therefore, we did a lot with the adults during the day. This included once going to their school to see it and the kids. Other days, we were out with one of the aunts going into the city of Quito, where I saw my first shrunken head. Was it real? I don't know but it sure was to me, and I didn't have a reason to think it wasn't. Why, you may ask?

We were told that in the mountains around us, there were head-hunter tribes that lived there, and you could hear the drumming. I believe the housemaids may have told us this. Also, everything would be fine as long as you could hear the drumming, but if it stopped, you should be afraid. One night, we were all hanging out in the bedroom where there were four girls sleeping, which included me. The bedroom had windows like you'd see in schools with the lower casement windows opening and closing only into the room. One of the maids was cutting napkins in half, as busy work I suspect, when suddenly we noticed no drumming sound. The next thing we knew, hands came through the windows grabbing at us, making us terrified, running around in fear. The grandfather didn't think what the maids had done was at all funny. The ladies got into some sort of trouble, but I couldn't help but realize how funny they were, and they were just playing with us without understanding how scared we were. The next day, I remember coming outside and the laundry was hanging up. They had been doing all the laundry and hanging the sheets out to dry. They were blowing and we kids were running through them, and the maids were chasing us and playing. I was used to seeing chickens everywhere outside and realized there were a lot less. I said something to the one Aunt Rene about it, and she said, "What do you think you've been eating?" God, how not used to this kind of living was I to this kind of living and how upsetting it could be and how it was the reality of how these folks lived, and it was normal. It was not normal to me, nor was I led to know what to expect, including the glaring differences. I sure did learn so quickly.

One day, we all went to an uncle's home which was a large wooded and unwooded farm with horses and all kinds of animals. Some were in pens and others, like the horses, which seemed to roam rather freely throughout the land area. We were riding and having fun, and it was my turn. Mind you, we rode bareback, and the uncle would call the horses by a whistle. It was so cool to see. I was on the horse, and we were starting to canter when suddenly he reared up, and I was suddenly being helped off him. Not a few minutes passed when we felt the ground beneath us shaking violently. That was my first earthquake, and it was a doozy, but thank goodness we were nowhere one would get hurt from much. The next earthquake was very scary, and it was closer to us finally leaving to go back home. You also have to remember it was the summer of 1970.

The family's Aunt Rene had a boyfriend who was an American helicopter pilot and was active at that time. I remember he had a bullet-wound scar on his side. But at this point, the Vietnam War was roaring. Also, throughout the time we spent there, there were as many changes in power in Quito, which was not always pleasant. I tell you this because on this day, we were trying to figure out how to make a cake at a high altitude. All of us were in the kitchen when all of sudden, we began to rock and shake. We ran outside and could see everything shaking, people getting down on the ground praying, glass falling off buildings.

As everyone was praying upward to the sky, we thought we were under attack. Terrified and not sure what to do, we just stayed outside watching all around us and what was happening. It was quite a shake too. Finally it subsided about ten or more seconds later with numerous aftershocks. When we went into the house, the upstairs was cracked pretty badly through the baseboards and some of the walls but were not unsafe. However, the damage in town near the city was massive. Glass had come out of buildings and destruction was intense to those homes that were not made so well. I have to admit I had scary moments like this that had left scars on my psyche throughout my life.

During those times, the kids I was with were with their mothers and extended families. I wasn't and came from a family that had taught you to keep your fears to yourself as those fears being known can and will be used against you. It was scary for me throughout the time I was there, and all I wanted to do was go home. It was there that I didn't like what we were living through, but at least I knew what to expect, whereas here in this foreign place I had to depend on myself, what I had learned so far in life, which wasn't much. I learned to understand a lot of Spanish real quick.

When I returned, my parents met us at the airport. I remember my mother's face, which was so happy to see me. I was thrilled to be home, as I called so often from South America due to homesickness.

She told me she had missed me so very much and that I was to sleep in my room with her that night. We had gone to bed when I heard a noise, and the dog was barking. My dad got up and we found that someone had tried to break into the house. My dad didn't have a clue what was going on and was squaring off at nothing or a phantom something in the upstairs hallway. I was yelling in Spanish to my mother. She kept saying, "Jeanne Marie, English!" And I finally came to enough to say someone was breaking in. She had heard it too, so I wasn't alone. Whoever it was left, and we did see remnants of them trying to break into the family room door. We acted as a team, a team of keystone cops, but a team all the same.

Life was calm for the first few weeks because it was appreciated that I was back home, and I loved being back. It wasn't too long before all became normal again, and they were at each other's throat day to day. The physical aspect of it became darker and darker, and I was getting scared my mother would get killed.

On the other hand, I had daydreams of my dad being taken out in a body bag, wishing for it all to stop. Due to my enmeshment with my mother, I protected her and wouldn't see my father's side of the equation then. But as I became a teen, I became belligerent and discovered marijuana by thirteen years old. That and the drugs I was given to lose weight by the doctor. I was numbing the pain of my childhood by this time but not with alcohol. Just marijuana and any other ingredients my parents had lying around. This included smoking cigarettes, theirs to be precise.

Chapter 2

In May of 1960, we were still living in Torresdale, Philadelphia, one of the furthest of the far-northeastern Philadelphia area on Pearson Avenue. I was born there in September of 1959. It was my mother's story consistently throughout my memory that she always wanted a girl and was going to have children until she had at least a girl. Therefore, after her having two boys, one very healthy red-headed boy, or my oldest brother, Tim, a.k.a. Timmy back then. Then two years later, Mom had Brian, and Mom had been exposed to measles during her pregnancy. Brian was born with serious lung problems and issues with his eyes. However, it wasn't an unusual issue in our family to have lung disease for various reasons. So Mom had her two sons, one who required a lot of attention due to medical issues. Even as a little nine-month-old, he was so sick. She said she almost lost him due to his breathing. Mom said that she realized she was pregnant with me because she couldn't stop eating grapefruit and other citrus and finally potatoes. I find it funny that to this day, I am allergic to citrus.

Mom repeatedly said how much she loved being pregnant and how much she felt that was her pinnacle in life. There was a day back when I was three, so it was 1962, that I was in the back seat of our 1963 rose-colored Galaxy 500. It was June 1 and I knew it was because it was little Timmie's birthday. He was gonna be seven. But see, Mom and Dad had a fight the night before. A bad one. The kind where she wears sunglasses and a bandanna, calling it a Jackie Kennedy day. So I had a bandanna and sunglasses on too, of course.

I was in the back seat while Mom parallel parked to the front of our brick duplex and said, "Jeanne Marie, get out the passenger side."

Well, there was an issue, which was my brother's birthday cake from Rilling's Bakery at 7328 Frankford Avenue that was resting on the passenger side well of the floor.

All I could say was "But, Mom…"

And she said, "Don't argue with me and get out now."

I sat there pondering how, and she wasn't listening as per usual, what to do. I had her screaming now and telling me I was being nothing more than a brat, so I stepped on the cake to get out of the car. She wasn't listening and I didn't see any other way out because there was no other way out. I don't remember much other than our neighbor, Mrs. Livolisi, coming out to tell her to stop. That was enough; it was only a cake and to stop. I don't remember much more from that one. Remember now, this is on a hot summer day in June in Philadelphia. My big brothers are in school at St. Catherines. Me, well, I was at home with Mom as I was not at school yet.

My main outlet was Miss Rose who came to clean our house. She was a wonderful African American woman who would come to our house and often would actually spend time with me as a young child. From memories being formed by my mother's consistent and continued need to repeat childhood stories to us became noticeably longer, and somehow, they'd change sometimes too. To this day, I wonder if my brothers noticed this issue.

My oldest brother is a great guy and a good family man with flaws like us all. The middle brother is a good family man too, just funnier. It is just not until now that I realized that I do not know them and why. I know I love them, their respective families too. I am proud of them all.

I just don't really know them.

But I digress again. Mom told me over and over throughout my life that her favorite time in life was being pregnant. Oh, she loved to chatter on and on about the elaborate escapades of her pregnancies and what happened and her deliveries with each of us. That was her one of three goals in life; one to be a mom and two to be a singer/entertainer and three not to ever be broke.

Ma said after delivering Tim that she realized he and she were alone as she reminisced with me that she had a conversation with him, something to the effect of *"I have no idea what I am doing, but I promise I'll do my best."* Mom said over and over how frightened she was because she felt so alone but exhilarated of having her child.

Mom explained, yet I don't know if it is even true, that after she had Tim, Dad took to his bed due to depression. He did rebound. Mom would say over and over she never had seen depression before. She said that there was one Saturday lunch that she decided to make a deli platter-type thing, and my dad flew off the handle and beat the hell out of her for the first time, and this was after Tim was born. I don't know how true it is anymore, but I do know she did withstand a good deal of physical/mental abuse later in life by him. However, her not ever experiencing or seeing depression or mental illnesses before was an abject falsehood and hers to be told unfortunately by acting out rather than ever admitting to it.

Mom always required help from her kids in ways that are not what most would expect unless you are the parentified child or the sick one. In addition, Mom wanted her kids to help protect her. Depending on our ages, depending on what we were going through, we experienced this decision to stay with a violent/narcissistic/bipolar-1/alcoholic father who lived in and out of Friends Hospital on Roosevelt Blvd. in northeast Philadelphia (yes, we visited our dad there too).

When Mom had to finally tell her mother-in-law, Edith Schmunk Callahan, no one to be fucked with on a good day, she tried to hit Mom. It was my aunt, my father's sister, Elayne whose real spelling is Elaine (she changed it, ugh who knows), who grabbed her hand and said no, stopping her from hitting Mom. At least that was how she described it. I can say that my Aunt Elaine/Elayne said it was true, so I guess it was. Sheesh, Dee Dee's (grandmother's nickname) li'l boy who was a grown man was in need of serious help, and she didn't want someone to know. Instead she'd rather bash the woman trying to help him. That, even in my understanding, made no bloody sense then, and I was only about three.

My aunt tried to explain that to her mother. My grandmother was perfect, and what was wrong with him, in her mindset, was all due to my mother, and that was that. But there was a whole lot that wasn't talked about, like Dad (my grandfather) saying he'd be better used as a greased pig 'cause at least he could've eaten him, but nah, there was no changing her mind. Both my aunt and my mother explained this to me over time too, to explain to me why she hated my grandmother so much.

Elaine/Elayne and Mom were very close. Although here is when I began to wonder about that because I don't ever remember her visiting my father when he was in the hospital in the sixties and seventies. My mother's children were born in 55, 57, and 59. Dad hit the mental health hospital and mental issues not long after.

It was at Friends Hospital (then private) when I saw a man with a lobotomy, wearing a half tie, drooling as he slid down the dinghy walls of the ancient wooden-framed walls painted with lead 1930s paint. All plain colors, nothing was warm, with furniture sort of willy-nilly placed clearly to line the walls and spaced apart so as not to have the egos too close to touch. I remember walking in, and Mom saying to me, "Stay near me and don't walk too far." Me in my green, short velveteen dress trimmed in lace, pixie haircut, and white patent leather shoes. Mom's hands were covered by her white gloves as she carried her puffy white and pink purse with hard handles and metal clasps to keep it shut in one hand and a small handkerchief in the other that she had just taken out of her purse. Then there was a female friend of my parents named Jean as well who appeared. The friend ran past my mother toward Dad as he descended the stairs. She was yelling, "Tim, Tim, I've missed you so much!" And started to laugh with my mother. I know she was playing, but Dad really didn't need that behavior. He didn't appreciate it and gave my mother a lot of guff over it, which was unnecessary as well.

Mom fundamentally refused to leave an abusive relationship for the same reasons my father left my mother—by acting it out in her pushiness and demandingness with expectation that she did all he asked. He'd make goal posts, and she met that goal post, and of course he'd lie and say that wasn't the goal post. At least that's how she explained it to eleven-year-old me. As I look back, they were both as bad as each other but in seemingly similar ways, for different reasons.

Chapter 3

Mom did elaborate that she was fearful of having a baby son as she had only been around baby girls her entire life. Being she was the oldest child of a family of five girls, she experienced everything her parents went through, and it wasn't pretty. Then she had another boy, and he was ill, needing a lot of attention due to his illness and cantankerousness and the fact that he wanted to be here. I came along two years later, and it wasn't too long after then apparently that Dad had his first in-patient stay at Friends Hospital in Philadelphia. So Mom had 3 children of which she was thrilled and not completely finished in her mind. Dad had done well through our one brother's illnesses, which were many; my middle brother is such a fighter.

Mom, as I said earlier, always wanted a girl. Oh, lucky me! The focus on a female child appeared traditional at first and, to me as a kid, something entrancingly unique. That's what made me so very different from everyone else in this house yet similar to that object of initial ineffective affection otherwise known as Mom.

At times, Mom was great with us as kids. She explored every holiday with us. This includes celebrating Lincoln and Washington's birthday separately. On Washington's birthday morning, we came to our morning breakfast plate with a paper hatchet filled with hard candy cherries. This was so cool to represent Washington and the cherry tree. Every birthday she'd make sure she sang happy birthday first to us. She also attempted to make Christmases as magical as she knew how, which was her absolute favorite holiday.

Mom loved music, which then included the Beatles and much more… Yes, it was a while ago. Mom's humor was always razor sharp and could kill you like a death by a thousand cuts. Dad wouldn't always get it and couldn't dance. Ya wonder what the hell did she marry him for… I did and as I got older and bolder and sick of things, I asked. And finally I got the truth. I will let you know what she finally did say in the end. She told me that she wouldn't marry anyone without the potential to make a good living. She wasn't going to live with someone who couldn't "take care of her." I asked her again, and she said the same thing—she'd never have married anyone that wasn't smart and capable of making a great income. She saw that in our dad and went for it. She should have had a clue as she met him in a bar. She was trying to get to the bathroom, and he was in the way and wouldn't let her pass because he was trying to chat her up. Well, it worked.

Yet Mom had worked until she gave birth with my oldest brother for the railroad in Philadelphia. She worked till she was in labor. Then she went back to work after I was in high school. Mom was an executive secretary for which she knew she was good. She did it all, including two kinds of shorthand. So much so that when she went back to work, her notes to us were half written in proper English and the other half in squiggles and scribbles of shorthand. I almost always had to call and find out what the hell she was saying to me. She found it funny every time she did it.

Sadly, Mom had a lot going on for her, which for her, she found it too much to cope with. Mom married a man, who, to botch my oldest sibling's quote, was more self-centered than she, and that's hard to beat. But she did. As much as my mother believed she was a loving mother and was forever more, she didn't understand the effect of her actions, and hence her life ending was a rough one, and for that I hate to see what she went through.

I realize as the daughter who couldn't handle the years of being told that Dad was fine until you were born, I peaced out with Mom in 1990. I still have one question about 1970 though. Why, seriously, why did my mother send me to South America with a family I barely knew, and I didn't want to go? That was not a place I really wanted to go, nor did I understand why I was going. Even back then I spoke with my neighbor, Maureen, who was my second mom, and she said she'd hide me in a closet, so I wouldn't have to go.

Maureen was a wonderfully energetic woman who was a mother of three and was very caring. She knew my household all too well as she befriended my mother as an adult and befriended me, at eight to nine years old, as another parental figure. She'd engage me in her household needs like cleaning and so on, but more than anything, she would get me to exercise, and I played with her kids. Her eldest was a boy, Jeff, and then Tracey and finally Heather. Now for her husband, George, he was a giant to me. He'd come in the house; I'd go out the back door. He just scared me due to his long hair, being tall, big, and handsome. I remember thinking his hands were *huuuuuuge*.

But there were times that my parents arguing was so bad, Maureen would let me just hang out at her house and called me a "mother's helper." I was like ten years old when this happened. I loved being needed and having an adult to talk to as well. Little did I know that she, too, was the youngest of three. I remember being totally shocked that she had a sister and a brother, but I digress. Anyway, Maureen's dad was an alcoholic at one point, and she told me her story about life as a young little girl who, of course, loved her dad. He'd threaten to walk into the water till his hat floated, meaning suicide. My father was threatening that often, especially when he was in depression of his bipolar disorder. So when my parents were really at it, and I hadn't really made friends with the girls in the neighborhood, she'd have me come over. She also liked to sew, and she'd have me sit with her while she sewed and the kids played. I felt loved and needed, which I didn't feel at home. I felt in the way and an annoyance because my mother was hysterically trying to keep her family together as sick as it was.

Even with my relationship with Maureen and her family, in the end, I had to go to South America (Quito), and I was only ten years old. I know, as an adult, after helping raise a few kids, working with loads of them too due to my job, that I wouldn't want my ten-year-old to go with a family we barely know to go to South America. Yes, they were our neighbors, but that was all. I hardly knew them, which consisted of parents and three kids. One boy and two girls, and I was their total opposite as I explained previously.

I tried really hard to fit in, but it just didn't happen. I loved being alone, playing with my pets, and dreaming. Dreaming of a life where I was important and connected to the family. Instead, I was the annoying kid who was always in the way of whatever parent I was attempting attention from, who was too busy. Mom said often, "You just needed too much attention." It wasn't until I was in my forties that I said to her that I was a child and children want and need a parent's attention, especially their primary caretaker, a.k.a. *mom*!

After returning from Quito, I did "play" with the girls across the street and their friends in the neighborhood. It was difficult for me because they'd do stuff I didn't understand. Most of the girls had sisters, and I only had brothers. It was a night-and-day kind of comparison between us. I liked sports, watching football and basketball. They didn't. But they'd play softball, jump rope, and the game of *it*. One day when I was eleven in April, I was playing it with the girls and fell because my knee shattered, and I couldn't move. My parents were fighting from the night before, and the day I fell was April Fool's Day, hence I remember the date. My knee was blowing up like a softball, and my mother took her sweet time coming over to me because she just didn't believe I was hurt. I could barely walk, and she argued with me to get up and walk. I did it by hobbling into the house. My dad was drinking but was still sober. In my house, whenever you were unwell or your arm was hanging off, you'd either take a bath or take a bath and even possibly do both. So she told me to take a bath. I got upstairs into the bathroom and took a bath, which swelled my knee even more.

I ran the bath, and my knee wouldn't bend. My mother was annoyed and bent it for me, where I screamed in pain. My dad came running into the bathroom, which he normally wouldn't have. He was an athletic guy as a young man, and he had bad knees. He saw what she had done to me and lost his temper with her, yelling and telling her that she made a bad situation worse. She and my dad began to argue, and all I could do was sit in a tub of lukewarm water, naked and uncomfortable that they were there, and cry. This happened on a Sunday, and I got in with the specialist that Monday. I had to deal with the pain all night and was so scared. We got there and my knee was seriously swollen. So much so that he had to drain about a pint of fluid off the knee. Then he did something I'll never forget because of the pain, for one, but because of the way he did it. He had to see if the "nerve" was still okay under my kneecap, which he didn't tell me. He normally would have done this with me alone, but this time, he demanded that my mother stay and watch because he couldn't believe that my parents didn't take me to the hospital for this injury. The doctor hit the nerve, and I hit the room screaming in pain. Mom yelled and cried saying how sorry she was to me. I cried and cried, telling her it wasn't her fault. I didn't like her crying as it made my heart hurt when she did, making me the greatest parentified child one could meet. The pressure became unbearable when I became an emancipated minor and had to escape from the pull of my enmeshment.

When I was about fourteen to fifteen years old, I had a friend, and she and I hung out a lot, smoking pot and enjoying the company of some guy friends. She had a boyfriend who was a marine, which I found weird. But I had a boyfriend too named Barry. Well, all he wanted was sex, and I was only fourteen and not ready, but he continued to push. He was five years older and, in reality, shouldn't have been allowed to be my "boyfriend." But my mother was so excited that I was going to the prom with him; she didn't seem to care. That and Maureen had tried to tell my mother that she was pretty sure that I was a lesbian. Mom wouldn't hear of it. To be honest, the way I found out was Barry's fault. He would take me out to dinner and do weird things like stare into my eyes, and all that did was make me uncomfortable. I was too young for what he wanted, but who was I gonna tell? He was sexualizing me, and I couldn't tell my family or anyone I knew. Then one night, he said, "Let's go to the movies." So he took me to a movie theater for dirty xxx-type movies. I was so confused until a lesbian sex scene came on. He was trying to touch me while the movie went on, and all I did was move him away, so I could see what the women were doing. I knew then what was wrong with me, and that was nothing. Nothing other than I liked women and not at all interested in sex with men, males, and/or boys at all. I could get what I wanted, do as I pleased with males, but I realized that I had an attraction to Vicky. But she was straight, and that was okay because I didn't know what to do yet. I just was too young to really know what I was doing other than longing for female company over males. Yet I continued to date males and went to four proms in my high school years.

One night in the early summer, Vicky and I had planned to go hiking the next day. I wanted to go and stay at her house and then go. I was upstairs in our kitchen when I was cleaning the stove off from dinner. I asked my dad if I could go and do exactly that—go to her house to go out the next day. I expected a yes, but Mom said yes, and my father yelled no. I got into it with my dad, and he took hot coffee grounds and threw them at me. I was so angry that my friend came into the house—she was a black belt—and went into a defensive position when my dad went to hit her, yelling at her to leave. My brother woke up and ran downstairs in his underwear, grabbing for me as my father and I tumbled into the living room. I had been hit, my clothes were ripped, and my ear had been pulled from the side of my head. My friend blocked a hit from my dad, and I got up running to her car, and my brother ran after me. We got into the car and took off to her house. This was not the smartest thing I did, but I was fourteen and angry, and I had just been attacked in my eyes.

I had no idea that my friend's father had been in Byberry Hospital for years due to his mental illness. He had been calling my parents, saying things to them about me and my friend. I met him when I got there, and her mom worked for the IRS. Her dad walked with two canes. He showed them to me and came with us to smoke some pot. I found this to be strange. He then showed his canes to me and pulled the handle wherein a knife came out the bottom. He said that it was easy to protect yourself. I was scared. He left and she and I got very, very high. Staying there that night, she went to school the next day, and I stayed back instead of going. I thought that they'd nab me at school.

I was right, and instead when school was over, the police showed up at her house. I stayed inside of the house while they used a bullhorn to try and get me out of the house. They had surrounded the townhouse apartment with lights blaring, trying to get me to come out past the doorway. They couldn't come in because it was a private residence, and they knew her father knew his rights. He had explained to me before this transpired that they couldn't come in under situations I was in. I was becoming progressively higher and higher and then another friend called me. This was unexpected that he'd call. He tried to talk me into going out to the cops, and I refused. I don't recall what happened so much as I was told that I did answer the door when they knocked on it a third or fourth time, and the detective grabbed me and put me in his car.

I woke up the next day in a mental hospital. At first I thought I was in prison because the windows all had bars on them. Then this girl stood over me as I opened my eyes.

She said, "Hi, I am Maryanne and I burn myself." Then she showed me her arms which were covered with burn scars on the inside of her arms.

I was totally confused, groggy, and just lost. I got up and pushed "Maryanne" away from me and walked into the hallway. There was a man standing in the hall with a dark beard looking like Cat Stevens, the recording artist.

I asked him, "Where am I and who are you?"

He answered, "You're awake, Jeanne, and you're in Horsham Hospital."

I was in total shock and asked a load of questions like what about school, what about my boyfriend, and my family, what's going on? The answers came very slowly at first wherein they did a medical workup on me, and suddenly I was in to see the psychiatrist. This was my first experience of mental health testing, which included my IQ Rorschach testing.

Finally, I was told what I had done the night before and that running away from home is against the law. The parents of my friend where I was staying kept my clothes from the night I ran off, and they were in a bag sitting on his desk. He said it appeared to him that I have a drug problem, but he knew of my father's mental health issues too. He then remarked how, yes, it could be a lot of my own fault and issues, but that the family sounds like a problem too, and that my clothing showed that there was a serious altercation. He couldn't know who was at fault. That was only partially how I ended up there. I tried their group sessions, and I had a roommate named Rae. I didn't know she had venereal disease. I found out the hard way.

After about a month there, I had earned a trip out of the hospital with a group of the kids I was in with, which was about twenty more kids. They ranged in age from thirteen to about seventeen. This was to be a run to the nearby mall. We went on a sunny early weekday afternoon. About six of us piled into the van to go to the mall. The fellow that was with us was a "MHT" or a mental health tech. We stopped by a building that I wasn't sure what it was. He told everyone he forgot something and wanted me to go with him. I was so trusting and went with him. The bastard raped me and then went back to the van, dragging me with him, threatening me the entire time. Who was I going to tell? No one would believe me. It was my word against his. I didn't realize that someone did care and did understand, and that was the psychiatric nurse that worked there. We got to the mall and met up with another person from the hospital who had three more kids with her. This was the psychiatric nurse. I stayed back, was quietly freaked out, and just kept to myself. We arrived back at the hospital, and she asked me gently and nicely what was wrong. I told her nothing. I just wanted a shower and to be left alone.

That night, I was asleep when I heard the door open. He had decided to work a double and kept following me from place to place. I smoked so he took me out to smoke, and he threatened me again. I just wanted to be left alone. There he was and I thought, *Shit he wants to do it again*, but it wasn't me he was after that night. He motioned to Rae, and she went with him. I followed them quietly into the general room where we all watched TV. There they were, having sex on a couch. I creeped back to my room and waited until the psychiatric nurse was back on duty to speak to her. When Rae returned to the room, I said, "What the hell were you doing?" And she said she had been having sex with him for weeks. I was so lost as to why, and she finally said he was her boyfriend. It didn't sit well with me, so I put in to speak with the psychiatric nurse for the unit. She came to me one morning directly after breakfast. I had to leave a conversation I was having with a girl named Rachel. She, too, admitted to him having relations with her as well. I knew I could tell the nurse about them but not about me; that'd make it too real. This was a difficult conversation because I didn't know where to start. She was so patient and pleasant that I finally told her what I had experienced with Rae, not myself though.

The next thing I knew, I was being brought into the head psychiatrist's office with the nurse. His office was beautifully appointed where you could see the grounds of the hospital. The grounds were quaffed and beautifully appointed. There was coffee and water sitting there. They asked me to sit. I was asked if I was okay and comfortable. Then he asked me about having a conversation with the nurse. I said yes and that I was sure she had already told him, so I felt that I didn't have to explain it all again. I was coming from confusion, fear, and shame, which had been there since childhood. I didn't know that as a young female, I had power and was already trusting in my higher self. It felt out of step from my age, which I didn't do all the time. He expressed how he needed to hear it from me and that there was nothing that was going to happen to me. I had no reason to believe him, but the nurse cajoled and was very supportive. I finally opened up to her, and he was there listening into the conversation. I explained what transpired with Rae, and the nurse took my hands and looked me directly in the eyes, asking if that had happened to me or Rae, and if not just Rae, to me too. She then explained that Rae was in the last stage of gonorrhea, and it was necessary to know about me, too, to keep me safe. I didn't want to say anything. I felt it was my fault. I was so scared, but I finally said what happened. I was terrified that I was going to be in trouble. All I knew was he was fired immediately after he was tested for gonorrhea

I tested negative and was so relieved. I wasn't pregnant either. Rae, however, was positive, and she was suddenly gone from the hospital the next day. No one ever said anything more to me about it. I was left to my own devices. That nurse quit and I was left with the rest of the MHTs, who ranged from their early twenties to their thirties at best. Most didn't have teens in their lives, so they really didn't connect to us. But one did try and found me a public defender for some reason who came to speak to me. I had been there a few months, and they said that they could help me. My time at the hospital, they noted, was with me trying to work it out with my parents. However, the circumstances as to how I ended up there, they felt I could become emancipated and move on from the family. I agreed thinking it was a great idea. I could move out and be an adult before I was sixteen years old. I also made friends with a couple of the MHT's males and females. But one was specifically known as Cinthyia Best who was the horticulturalist for the place, working with us kids and was an out lesbian. Her roommate was once married to the king of a motorcycle gang. They were just friends, and I knew this as we chatted at length.

So I was hospitalized after running away from the constant fight between the narcissists fighting for power in the facade of a wealthy-ish household. I left my blood-related family in 1975–1976 when I was deemed an emancipated minor. Says a lot about our relationship today. Back then in the seventies, this was not considered a family issue; it was "her problem," meaning my issue. Now I was on my own legally but not emotionally, or my internal world still had a combination of my father-and-mother hierarchy that, without my realizing, I was following crunchy old rules that weren't helpful. I had support from these MHTs and, in time, was invited to their house and met Cindy's lover, Pat. It was my first crush, and I could hang out from time to time, and I never made a move until I was emancipated. So I was finding my sexual identity as I had no idea what lesbian meant until I met these women. I felt like I was home.

But I digress a bit… At this time, I was appointed an attorney or the typical public defender, and my parents engaged one too. It was our neighbor who represented another person against my mother years before for a car accident. My father hated this guy. When we moved from Torresdale, he came across the street and introduced himself as Burt Felgoise, and my dad threw him out. So you can imagine my surprise when Mr. Felgoise came to me and tried to talk to me about going back home without a court case. I basically did the same thing as Dad had done years before and ceremoniously dismissed him.

The day of the hearing, my parents were there, and the judge was seated after being introduced. The MHTs I mentioned were there as support too. My mother stood up to speak, and he told her to shut up and sit down. I was so taken back from it, and I felt so bad for her. I didn't want to go back to that house without having some sort of balance of power. I felt the need to protect Mom that day and started to stand when suddenly the lawyer said to me, "She's the opposition, Jeanne. You have to suck it up." At this time, I was still blaming my father for all he did as the only reason our house wasn't a home. Remember, Dad was a lawyer, but he sat quietly while Burt Felgoise argued for my parents. Remember, the clothing that I wore that night when I left home was bagged up by my friend's mother. That bag was brought out to the courtroom. Blood was on my shirt, my pants, and my sweater. It looked horrible. This won my case immediately. He assumed that I was happy about winning, and I was, but I was terrified too. What was next? Where would I go, and what would I do? I went back to the hospital for the night.

The next day, I went to their house and was considered an adult. I was allowed to smoke in the house now but was warned that if I smoked pot in the house, they'd throw me out. I agreed. Also, I had one credit left to finish school, so I had to finish school but needed to find work, which I did immediately at Richardson and Merrell (the Vicks VapoRub company) in their canteen.

Instead of the family being broken, the black sheep syndrome was easier, and that's where Mom unburdened her shame of having a lesbian child she deemed fat. My grades had plummeted, and my middle brother was struggling, needing some tutors. He is an incredibly gifted man, a genius in fact. Our oldest brother was leaned on as brother/head of household by the time he was twelve or even younger.

I continued to live with my family very separately for about a month when I met a twenty-three-year-old man named Jim. We dated for about two months when I, at sixteen, moved in with him, and my parents couldn't do anything about it. Living with Jim was fun at first. We lived in a small apartment where he had a waterbed. I worked at the same time he did, so he drove me to work daily. I started buying things for myself for the first time, which were household items, including Japanese paintings and nothing too shoddy either. I thought this could work, but there was one issue. I knew I was a lesbian and not so interested in his desire for "nightly activities." We played happy family for about a month when I realized that my items went missing. Anything that I'd have purchased, including a Japanese silk painting, was no longer in the house. James was selling anything I had for drugs. I didn't realize it as he knew I wouldn't be the "one" to marry him. His brother married a fourteen-year-old with her parents' good wishes, and he thought he'd do something similar with me. I told him that I preferred women, and he still wanted to stay with me. But I didn't realize it because he wanted to use me for what I could financially support. I left him one night by walking down a road at about 2:00 a.m., looking for a telephone booth to find help.

My father answered the phone and demanded I stay where I was. It wasn't safe there, so I moved on, and I was weighing whether or not asking for help was a smart thing. I had no place to go, and he was willing, so I called again in a safer area. When they got me, not a word was spoken until we arrived at the house. My dad kept asking me if I could be pregnant. That's all he seemed to ask, rather than "Are you okay?" or "Did he hurt you?" Maureen did come in and asked, and I was able to explain that I wasn't pregnant, but I had been used and used badly. I also had to go to work the next day, and he worked there. What was I supposed to do? Eventually my mother asked if I was okay, and I was told I wasn't working there anymore because that was where he worked. I never saw him again.

It appeared that I graduated from my actions of using drugs (mainly marijuana) and running away to a hospital. It is my truth that I need to transcend, and these are the beliefs I've had of myself, which are completely unfounded but were instead infused. I am letting them go, so I am finally, at sixty-three, free from the psychic bonds of childhood that idiotically I thought were gone. I suddenly had clarity and recognition as to why I had accepted the black sheep emblem Mom emblazoned on my soul.

In that place, Horsham Hospital, it was twofold, good and bad (I know, very black-and-white thinking). The hospital helped me get my emancipation (emancipated minor) from my parents. But I was raped by an employee there. Because he raped someone who had gonorrhea, the psychiatric nurse there, who was someone I remember was White, asked, and I was amazed then that she was married to a Black man who ran the TLA in Philly. She approached me after the rape because I shared a room with the girl he was molesting nightly. He raped me on an outing, and it wasn't pretty, and it isn't to be discussed here. But the point is, I learned a whole lot there. I was released and finished high school at another school during the summer because I only needed one more credit to complete school by sixteen years old. I'd graduate with my class. *Oooops*, or would I?

Dale Goldman, Lisa D'auria, Hope Blatt, and a few others from my school had found out where I had been. I was told a stupid story that it was the school's mistake for an overheard phone call. Then I found out that it was my mother telling someone where I was and why? Because she needed to talk. She had a sick, mentally ill husband who wasn't coming home and beat the shit out of her when he was there. She had a daughter going off the rails and now announced she was a lesbian.

Oh, Lordy, my life is badly falling apart. I stood up to that school and said, "No, I will go through with this," and now I know how much my dad had to do with that happening too. Yes, my dad was a jackass bastard and a nasty piece of work most of the time, and he did good things too. Like our mother, our father too wasn't all good or all bad; they're a lot of both. However, I have to fill in some "blanks" that are important for me to unburden. I am sure you feel I have done that already. I have to, to a degree. My dad, being a lawyer, let them know what quagmire the school would be stepping into if I were not to graduate as all others did, which was through the ceremony. I wasn't sure that I wanted to do this and expose myself to ridicule. I took the ridicule and raised them disregard for their opinions and moved on. I walked up with an attitude and defiantly grabbed my diploma.

Chapter 4

You'd think I would go off to college as both my brothers did. I went to the National School of Health Tech. I, of course, didn't choose it; my mother did. Here I was to study nutrition, but of course, my mother liked it I believe because back in 1978, I was dressed like a nurse with the nurse's cap and all. Mom had always wanted me to be a nurse. Not a doctor, a nurse. I didn't want to be second to anyone, which I saw as being a nurse (so incorrectly). I wanted to be a doctor, but she and Dad thought I wasn't bright enough, whereas whatever Tim wanted, he got.

He was first premed and didn't like it and quickly changed to being prelaw. Dad became a complete jackass to him too. My father's narcissistic personality was so glaring, and his jealousy was even worse. I was in my room, and I could hear the conversation between my brother and Dad. My father, without a reason or a discussion, just verbally plowed into Tim when he transferred to pre-law. He ranted and raved how he'd never be as good as he is and that he'd be nothing compared to what he accomplished. Nice guy, eh? Mom didn't say that to Tim, but she would defend Dad's statements. I know how because he did the same to me. The only one that could do no wrong was Brian. He was the family favorite even though we teased about it. It was reality. It hurt us all. Brian wanted to be a journalist, a musician, and more. They moved heaven and earth to get his needs met, including Mom paying off his student loans. I certainly would love to have that kind of help, but it was never to be. But Brian wanted to be a musician, and he got support for going to school and his music. I got second best, if at all. My family heard that I was a lesbian and was seeing women but was cruelly overmothered and was used to not being heard.

Mom's mother wouldn't help. Mom said that her mother was done babysitting and that she was not there to be helping out with her children's children. She said that Dad was so in love with having his boy, and boy you could tell by the unequal number of baby pictures between the three of us. Tim was adorable, and Dad had huge smiles on his face. Dad's mother was happy to take over, and Mom said she wasn't going to have that at all. They fought constantly over the years, and a lot of it was over the kids. As I got older, whenever they fought, it was me my mother would grab and take with her when they were fighting. It was horrible and sometimes scary. Nights were not fun no matter how often you may believe it didn't happen. Growing up in our home was no joke.

Manipulation and lying wasn't unusual in my house. There is a difference now only because I can see it, and now I have a choice whereas then I hadn't. But when I was in the mix of it, I didn't and probably couldn't because I truly believed my job was to make her happy and to keep her safe. A lot to take in for a little kid, and I was the model parental child in the family as was Tim, my oldest brother. Our middle brother was not well most of his childhood. Mom had to spend time with him due to his issues. It was understood that he was sick with asthma and other life issues.

By the time I was eight years old, we had experienced approximately four hospitalizations for my dad, him almost losing his job, and moving to a ritzier part of Pennsylvania, outside of the Northeast Philadelphia area, wherein I felt ripped from the only place I ever felt safe to a place that didn't resemble a fun place to live. At least in Torresdale, we'd have a fight and play the next day. We'd be outside for hours with the neighbor kids and have lots of fun. This new place was supposed to have a better school system with a bunch of up and coming middle-aged parents who could say that they "made it" in terms of societal norms.

I believe my mother pushed my dad into this, and he had to carry his family and do well financially. This was way too much for his mental health, and he deteriorated slowly in front of our eyes, but we didn't know that. He was sexualizing everything, becoming embarrassing out in public, and we no longer brought friends home because of the tensions in the house. It was so bad with our mother that, at times, no one wanted to be first to get into the house for fear of what mood Mom might be in. We could tell it wasn't going to be good just because of the night before. I remember being so sleepy at school and almost falling asleep once, and the teacher threw an eraser at me and called me a spoiled brat. Very unhelpful to be honest.

Life in our household was not for the faint of heart. My parents' arguing was sometimes funny. One time my dad accidentally broke a pot, and Mom acted like it was an act of high treason! By the time they were done arguing, the $5 pot was a $50 pot, and it was near irreplaceable. I remember watching this argument as if it were an auction, and Mom was winning.

My parents arguing was intense and violent, which became dangerously close to homicide as time progressed. Dad's violent tendency was almost maniacal at times. He'd hit her, and she'd take it. Black eyes and swollen cheek. The next day, she'd do what she normally would do, and he'd go to work like nothing ever happened if it were during the week. If it were the weekend, it would continue into the next day if he remembered. As time progressed, these fights were between him and each of his kids. Sad to say, we all had to defend ourselves from his attacks on Mom and defend ourselves at times. I know he had it out with each brother, and I will only describe how it was for me.

One summer, my mother and father had fought, and Mom decided we—meaning she and I—would leave the house to go to Cape May, New Jersey, where we had friends that owned a motel. Mom rented a car, which was her first experience of power brakes. Oh my god, I had a headache before we got down the street as she kept hitting the brakes so hard that I'd go flying. I was about thirteen years old. We left the boys behind, which was their decision, not hers. She told them not to tell him (Dad) where we were. We left on a weekday and got to the seashore, which I absolutely loved. Mom and I and the family who owned the motel hung out for a few days, which was where I got drunk for the first time in my life. Yes, I was only thirteen and got totaled on Tia Maria. I was a lightweight at thirteen and went to bed early because I got sick. I remember my thoughts were that my head was going to fall off if I didn't sit up with all the pillows in the motel room. Mom tried to get pillows back for herself when she came in, and I said no. My head would fall off for which she laughed at and grabbed them anyway. I immediately threw up on her. I didn't really drink again until I was in my early fifties.

So Friday came around and Dad called her at the motel and knew where we were because my brother or brothers did tell him where we were. Of course he was coming down and not letting her have a good time and not him. So he took a train from Center City, Philadelphia, to Cape May. After his phone call, I became scared that he'd act out when he arrived there.

He came down to the motel, and all seemed okay in front of everyone, but he was slowly getting drunker and drunker. He went to bed after becoming nasty and ugly in front of the folks who owned the motel. I wanted to go to bed and had no reason why I couldn't or shouldn't go in the room because he was probably asleep. My mom stayed downstairs hanging out with her friends. He woke up and was vile toward me, and I wasn't going to let him hit me like he hit my mother. He went to punch me, and I somehow pushed his punch past me and grabbed his belt, throwing him across the room into the chairs near the windows. I ran out of the room, and he stopped at the door. He may have been drunker than drunk, but he knew not to chase me into public. Dad cut his head and finally passed out.

The next morning, he woke up and got me up to go get coffee down the street. I said no and he was confused. He came back into the room and asked where he had gotten the cut from. He hadn't had one memory of the night before. I now knew how it worked. Drunken behavior and blackouts acted as an excuse for horrible behavior and abusiveness.

The fighting was incredibly violent and, at times, would be very scary. It was so violent that I still struggle to sleep at night to this very day. I am lucky to get three full hours of sleep. Mom's understanding of this issue was my "anxiety," which I do have, but she assigned it to just anxiety as if it was a diagnosis that covered everything because her uncle had it. She didn't see how badly she had it, ever. Mom wanted me to be her confidant, take her side all the time, even in adulthood. When I wouldn't, she'd say, "What about me?" She'd say that a lot throughout my life.

But living in this household was not for the faint of heart. For example, when I was only ten years old, I was a shy, scared kid when my parents made arrangements for me to go with our neighbors to South America, their home country. The mother's sister was getting married, and they had three kids our ages, but I didn't get along with the girls and only was friendly with their son who was much older than I. Nevertheless, I ended up going to Ecuador for months in the summer of my tenth year. I had my period since I was nine, so this wasn't going to be a fun place for me when I got it as it was painful and ridiculously long. I was so embarrassed by it because I was so young and having it was supposed to be secret, quiet, and not discussed. Having to wear pads and belts were bulky, and I had the shit taken out of me for the paper tail sticking out when I was playing flag football with the boys. I stopped doing this with the kids I knew. But my parents, during a drunken evening with the neighbors, made arrangements and decided to send me without including me in the loosely called *their* process. I wondered often if my brothers felt this way, but I never really knew. As I am writing this now, I still don't know. At sixty-three, I feel painfully mixed with loss and bereaved love, anger and resentment. The kind of bereavement where I felt the loss to what could have been as siblings. The reason I write about all this now isn't to say what Mom did was all bad, and she was horrid; she wasn't all that. She was unashamedly Jean Maude Caudle Callahan, daughter of Louridna Saunders and the most wonderful daddy in the world, Herman Caudle. Well, that's how Mom told it most of the time to the general public or to those that cared to listen, ad nauseam!

As a young child, I believed every word my mother said; every single syllable that dropped from her lips was golden law. She was also, in my eyes, the most beautiful woman. I loved my mother to the ends of the earth, and she was mine. She would talk about her life to me from the time I was a little tiny thing, and it wasn't until I was in my sixties did I realize what a horrible impact it had on my life. Not everything is meant for a child's experience, and yet I know, truth be told, she didn't know any better.

The difference now is I can see, whereas then it was unseen manipulation. Therefore, I hadn't had choice. Now I not only have a choice, but she has chosen to live the repercussions of her choices. I am aware those choices are made from fear and for self-preservation and have nothing to do with me or anyone else for that matter. At this point in my writing this, my mother was dying in Pennsylvania while we, my wife and I with our three fur babies, picked up sticks and moved to North Carolina. Even in her dying time, she made it very evidently clear, by making eye movements and guttural responses to that fact, that we weren't willing to do what she wanted, which was to sit and wait while she died. It was insanely hard to make that decision, that realization that I had to stay with my truth no matter what mom's decisions were. Her death was her way, and my ability to cope or not cope was mine, and I am learning to accept that part.

It is here where I must explain that I have some interesting memories that are, let us say, rather young. I would be eight to nine months old during this incident that I confirmed with my mother and had her confirm this with my wife. At this age, I distinctly recall a man who I thought was ironing something in my small bedroom and would reach into a box and hand me the most humongous cookie, the size of your head.' Mom later explained he was the wall-paper hanger, and I said yep, I remembered pink ballerinas on the wall. She said those giant cookies were normal-sized gingersnaps, my favorite. But from a little person's perspective, they'd be huge. Who says we don't lay down memory tracks a little is just plain wrong. It is no surprise really. My early memories of myself as a young child between crawling and walking was like when I got out of my wooden playpen jail,… It is no surprise really. My early memories of myself as a young child between crawling and walking was like when I got out of my wooden playpen jail, as per usual, and headed toward the yelling I heard. I saw handbags floating through the air aimed toward each parent. I got scared and was scared, and my father hit her, and it was over. Now I know that it means I was between ten and thirteen months old with what I saw. What a lovely childhood memory to ask your fifty-three-year-old mother about. She said she didn't remember it, and it probably didn't happen. When I had the chance to ask Dad, he had diagnosed Alzheimer's, which I believe was Korsakoff's (a form of dementia induced from alcohol abuse). However, he did say these things, but because as with all forms of dementia, they have moments of clarity.

Truth is, I don't know.

Dad said, "I do know. She said something, as per usual, like I wasn't doing enough or being enough." Just like what my mother would say. Then "She wondered why I'd throw shit at her. Your mom is a piece of work, ya know. But you two are thick as thieves. Hated the both of you."

I walked away with the normal feelings of the warm and fuzzies as would you, of course. By then I was in my thirties, living through my years with the best therapist I had ever been with, so I could handle the continued and prolific abusive behavior. Plus, I hadn't seen my dad in about nineteen years, so it was only to be expected yet a complete and utter letdown.

By then my dad was in the fullness of dementia. It was more probable Korsakoff's, but he was diagnosed with Alzheimer's. As I mentioned before, no one took into account the years of alcohol abuse he sustained, and what it did to help him survive his childhood, teens, and adulthood did a number to his intellect. He was at one time a very smart man. He loved being a history teacher, which he did while he went to law school at Temple University. Dad went to night school and held down a job after he married Mom. However, he was married to a woman that even his parents didn't know because they married in secret. Why? Well, Mom was pregnant out of wedlock during the 1950s. His parents and her parents would have had a fit and wouldn't support this marriage. At least his parents wouldn't have accepted it at all. Why again? Mom was not Catholic. But she was pregnant with my eldest brother. Even more, his sister had been married to a non-Catholic and had a child, my incredible cousin. But they acted the same about Dad marrying Mom. I don't know why but Mom said that it had to do with my grandmother's need to keep her perfect son close to her, and no one could match up to her expectation of a wife for him. Unfortunately, she was right.

Not my mother, my grandmother was right. She couldn't live up to his expectation, nor did she to hers. Neither were happy with each other, yet they stayed married for thirty-two friggin' years. They fought so much that it was amazing there was never a homicide. The intensity that we endured of our parents' physical abuse of each other was such that it was normal to see Mom with black eyes and more. Then one day in the mid 1980s, my mother hit my dad with a frying pan. Yep, a real live big-ass, heavy frying pan.

They had moved to Center City, Philadelphia. They sold the house in Montgomery County, Pennsylvania, to move into the lovely City of Philadelphia. Mom cried so hard that day they moved, and she struggled to talk sometimes. But Dad wanted to move smack dab in the middle of the city, in a high-rise building that dad's bank was involved with financing. It was called the Academy House back then as it sat over directly next to the Academy of Music. It's a huge high-rise. It was a three-bedroom condominium. This was *not* a great experience for any of us. I don't think we lived there very long as a family at all. I would come by now and then because I was involved with a woman in the building and living was with her then in a cult called Direct Centering. Brian lived there, and Tim was in law school by then.

Then one night, Mom finally hit back, or she'd like you to believe that, but Mom gave as good as she got. Mom was not able to accept my father's mental illness, which was intense for anyone to have to live through, let alone have a family with him. It's been said by Tim, my brother, that Mom was the most narcissistic person ever until she met Dad. Mom set Dad off a lot. She'd push him and not really hear what it was he was saying, which was when he couldn't think. And his trauma of childhood drove his adulthood, and that was something Mom just thought was hogwash. So on the day she hit him with the frying pan, it was 8:00 p.m., and she called me.

I was nineteen years old by then, living with a woman named Linda who was thirty-three. She was an accomplished musician, singer, and teacher when we met. I was just very emotionally young.

When I got the phone call from my mother this particular night, she was frantically calling my name, saying she needed me "right now!" So I went up to their apartment, and there was my mom frantically standing over my dad, trying to see if he was feigning being dead. I came in and there was my dad lying on his side next to the bed in their bedroom. All I could think to do with my nineteen-year-old brain was to get a mirror Mom had and bring it to his mouth to see if he was breathing. He was and Mom was relieved. I was crazed with "What did you do?" No! I mean, I railed at her "Really, what did you think you were doing?" I mean, it would make sense if she had hit him in the kitchen or somewhere even closer to where a frying pan would have been, but this was way far away from there. That meant to me that she had time to think about whatever he said or did and went back in her rage and hit him with his back to her, otherwise he wouldn't have been on his side with his back toward the bed and his head toward the wall.

By the time I got him up, he had a lump on his head. He then voided everything everywhere, which was so much fun when it was your dad, to help him through this because he was drunker than drunk and had been injured. He couldn't get his bearings and argued a bit, but I changed him and put him in bed. Now I know I should have taken him to a hospital, but I didn't know that then, nor did I really care anymore about either of them. They fought this way my entire life, and I hadn't lived with them for quite a bit. I was so used to keeping secrets that I figured I just get on with it. The entire time I was cleaning up Dad, I had no idea where she, Mom, went. I found her in the kitchen, walking around, chatting to no one, but she was speaking out loud. She said, "You can't tell anyone!" and I was think-ing, *Who fucking cares!*

I had to finally then say it and said to her, "Mom, no one gives one flying shit what you two do. I just don't get it anymore, but I am done."

My mother kept crying and saying she didn't mean it to which I said I knew she thought she didn't mean to do it, but she did, and it was as bad as her deciding not to let him drown in his turtle soup when he passed out in it. Yes, he could have drowned in his own soup, but she thought she had better not as they were in Nassau, and she didn't know what could happen to her. Yep, to her.

As we, the children, grew up, we all had our turn with our father too. He squared up to each of us one time or another. By then Dad didn't have a clue who he was, and he lived the life of the bipolar who loved his life in the high and drank through the depression.

Finally, he found someone during a year or so at University of Pennsylvania. He met his second wife. As time progressed, Dad said that Charlie, the second wife's son, was Dad's son. God knows that till this day, I don't have a clue. I do know that Charlie said the same thing to me too when Dad married his mom. That's why my father gave a set of cuff links that sort of had his and Dad's initials on them. Charlie was old enough that he was working and was an engineer of some sorts with computers. He was aiming to get married when I met him and his mom. She was nice enough, but I never ever accepted her as my stepmother because I had a mother, and back then in my mind, not a soul could fill those shoes. No one, even as a stepparent.

In the end, he was small, a little feeble, and none of those things I saw as a child. The big man I knew once until I was about eight was gone. However, now I can see he had been gone since the Friends Hospital in Philadelphia. They took my father and burned his brains into nothingness. He was no longer the human who he started as. My dad had to cope with multiple hospitalizations wherein the psychiatrists of the time recommended shock therapy. Think clearly here, this was from the late 1960s through the 1970s. Dad had multiple rounds of pernicious shocks. Once he had as many as twenty-plus sessions in a day. *A day!*

Sadly, and I know this sounds cold, it was her absolute choice. She didn't have to go this way, and I hated to see it even as I was very angry with her. Later I'll explain how we were able to make peace. At least I was.

Chapter 5

At this point, I met a woman who said she was straight but wanted to experience a lesbian relationship. She was named Helene LaMare, whose real name was Helen Falcone. She was half Italian and half Jewish. My mother despised her, calling her ugly and "only after your money." What money? I had no money.

I worked at three restaurants while going to school part-time at a community college. Nothing ever made sense, and Helene was not ugly, unique but not ugly. She used me for a while, and I was a willing participant until it came crashing down. We had a group of friends including gays and lesbians, trans and more. We often would have parties and give them a theme, like the "Caribbean Garden Party" for which we had a blast of a time. In fact, that was where I met Helene as she was a friend of Gary's, and he knew her for a long time considering what we considered a long time in our twenties.

Life became wilder and wilder with the people we'd meet and hang out with in the "gayborhood" of Philadelphia. The clubs ran all night, and you could go out early and leave in the morning, take the subway, and get to work on time. This, of course, was without sleep and a quick Swish washup before going so you didn't stink like a brewery with a huge dance floor and cheap aftershaves. But that relationship with Helene became violent for some reason, and now from thirty thousand feet and years, I can see she was a representative of my parents. She started getting involved in a cult group called Direct Centering, which was a false game plan of how to get whatever you want. Because by using double-talk, you already have all you've wanted. If you accept what you have as your needs being met, then you are not lacking anything and, in truth, "have all you ever wanted." It never flew with me too well, but I was concerned about what she was doing and why, hence I joined it thinking I could be the White knight in shining armor and save her from herself. Hmmm, what was I thinking with as it was not based in reality? I thought it was.

I met these guys a little at a time, and they came from everywhere—Florida, Philly, and NYC. The main base was in NYC. We all worked hard and played harder. Getting involved in Direct Centering was so dangerous though. I had stopped using drugs by now and noted that the folks I was friendly with were beginning to use. Mind you, this was time of just knocking on the door of GRID, gay-related immune disease. Later it would be renamed HIV and AIDS. So many of us were afraid of getting sick, but we weren't sure how it was transferred from person to person. Of course they made it a gay-related disease, so no one really cared until they cared because that was a stupid concept. Reality still is, gay people hide themselves for the reasons of society and bring home to straight society, where they hide these diseases. Sad but true.

We were a diverse group of about one hundred or more individuals, ranging from young teens, a.k.a. baby dykes and pool boys, to elderly folks that we could connect with around the gayborhood. They tended to own businesses like bars and restaurants, antique shops, and of course the most famous hangout—Giovani's room. Newspapers, books, music, jewelry, and more of the openly gay and lesbian were found here. We traveled a lot between Philadelphia, New York, and Baltimore. There were a lot of people going to the village and more, and we had a great time, but there were some seriously bad times too. Especially when someone was in trouble, like being held up and the cops wouldn't help. I had more friends who cross-dressed during that time and were often beaten up, even pistol whipped, left naked, and alone in an alleyway.

Also, at this time, there was a separatist movement separating gay men's needs not being met to that of lesbian needs. It is no different than in a straight life, wherein the distribution of wealth is men first and women not second but *last*. I personally never ascribed to it because I had boys in my family whom I loved. I questioned women having babies that if they had a male child, would they be "separatist toward them?" That would start arguments as it was noted as comparing apples and oranges, and to this day, I do not see it this way at all. Nothing is so black and white as separatism, and it is no different than the era of Jim Crow in my opinion.

This insidious disease did help disassemble some, if not most, of this bigoted ideal. People were dying at such rates; just being diagnosed was a death sentence. It was a scary time, yet breast cancer was still killing women at a similar rate, and no one got too hot under the collar for this. When it was figured out that HIV/AIDS was sexually transmitted along with other body fluids, more and more information about the truth began to come out. Africans had suffered this disease for many years prior to the outbreak in the USA. It was called the slims due to such weight loss then death follows. This sadly is what helped pull this weaponization of this disease to the reality of what it is, and it is an equal opportunity killer. *But* while living through this, even my mother would demand I stay away from clubs and friends, so I didn't get it. Don't eat the food or drink the drink, you'll die. I am not going to say I was not concerned. I really was, especially the development of the dental dam (look it up). That would have killed lesbian sex.

I had a friend who had been diagnosed, and when he found out, he went out to California and had sex with anyone anywhere as he knew he was dying. But he took so many with him, and for that, I am forever angry with him. I also know that I am not him and not as scared as he was at that time. It must have been terrifying.

Within about five months, we lost fourteen people to AIDS. It was devastating and destroyed our fight for our rights because so many said we were getting what we deserved. Then the babies and straight folks finally started to leak into the American culture; the innocents were dying. When you are a member of the LGBTQI community, it was your choice, your fault. The saints during this time were the women and gay men as usual. Caring for those so sick that they couldn't care for themselves, and their families wouldn't.

I remember being at a party where I brought someone with me from the AIDS support group. No one knew as it was no one's business, of course. We ate and played, and a friend was selling insurance.

I say friend loosely here. When he spoke to my friend, he asked him about his insurance needs, which at that point he had none. No car or house or job.

So he said to him, "How do you live?"

And he told him.

Well, the house shook when this guy started yelling, telling everyone, "Don't eat the food or drink anything, this faggot has AIDS!"

He continued to scream at me for about ten minutes, and the poor guy with me was hiding behind me, saying he was sorry. I threw the jackass out and told anyone who wanted to believe this guy's bigoted sickness that they could leave too. Many left and I never saw them again. I continued as a support worker and didn't leave him. He was so broken by it, and all I could do was listen to him. I was embarrassed, but I wasn't dying as he was being treated like a second-class citizen. Thing is, he was straight and got it through drug use. He did laugh saying he never had been called a faggot before, but hey, there's always a first time. I wanted to melt into the wall. I was so upset by that behavior.

Men and some women were dying so quickly from onset to death. Also, women were dying at high rates of breast cancer, which wasn't being looked into any differently than HIV/AIDS until some years later.

People did their best believing that being vegan was good, not being vegan was good, exercise helped, or it didn't. Then there were drugs starting to come out that did help for some for a bit of time, and we all learned more about blood, T cell counts, and more than we ever thought we'd have to when we were in school. Dr. Ift came through with a great deal of help for the afflicted. This was our eighties pandemic, and it was scary.

I met Shawn and Toni during this time, and they were best of friends. I initially met Shawn on the train going to and from work. We went out on a date and then a little more of a date and enjoyed each other's company. Her ex was still living in the apartment building, which was at times weird, at the very least. Then one day, I met Toni. She had been broken up after twelve years with a woman named Francha. You guessed it, I got together with Toni almost immediately. It didn't help Shawn and Toni's friendship at all. But we got together, and I found her to be loving, caring, and crazy goofy with a lot of opinions. What I loved was her desire for family and how much she loved her nephews, one of whom she was raising.

Over time, we moved in with each other, and I found out that Toni was cheating on me after about a year. However, I was not broken up about it as this woman had two children, and I could see she'd be happier. I would be happier still growing up as I was fifteen years her junior.

Or so I thought I'd like to find a younger woman. Instead, I met this gorgeous woman at my job named Kathy. She could speak five languages, was a mathematician, and was fully skilled in data work. She was Portuguese, African American, and British. Tall, lanky, smart, and beautiful. I found any reason I could to talk to her and found she was doing the same thing. But my friends, all of whom were Caucasian, were a bit taken back by her being a Black woman. One of my friends said she couldn't be my friend anymore if I continued to be with her. I never took ultimatums and haven't spoken to her to this day. Now Kathy and I talked for a few weeks and then started dating. After about a lesbian year, a.k.a. three months, we moved in together, and I was so happy.

She worked hard and played hard, and I didn't know how mentally ill she was until about eighteen months into the relationship. She started drinking, and it went downhill from there. Toni kept getting in touch with me, saying she made a mistake and wanted to come back to me. I wanted to be *alone* and had enough. In the middle of all this, my dad called and said he was getting married. I had an excuse to leave for Florida and get away from all of it. I felt so overwhelmed with too many relationships at one time. So much drama, or so I thought. Family drama is effing worse.

Chapter 6

I hadn't heard from my father in about two years at this point and was confused that he wanted me to go to his wedding. It was later that I found out that I was the only one from his family that attended, which I found sad.

I left for the wedding and was happy to be on my own. I spent a week in Winter Park, Florida, in a hotel. Dad's soon new to-be wife didn't want me to stay there. Nice, eh? At least I got to see the family cat that my father stole from us and brought to Florida with him. His wife painted pictures of him. In fact, she only seemed to paint pictures of cats. I got creeped out when I saw that the ceiling of their bedroom was completely mirrored by cheap long mirrors.

I knew my dad was a freak, but I certainly didn't need to experience it. I was so glad I was staying in a hotel nearby. Apparently, her son was there too. His name was Charlie and was aged between Brian and me. He had his fiancée with him to the wedding. Dad treated him like a son, giving him a wedding gift of gold cuff links that were engraved with his initials. They were nice enough when I was with my dad and his wife, but I was uncomfortable. They hung back with me one evening after the practice dinner and started to talk a lot about how my dad knew his mother and for how long. I had thought he met her in the hospital but found out that wasn't true. They'd known each other for twenty-two years, and Charlie was twenty-one. I was twenty, and I was getting the hint as he kept looking at me and shaking his head yes.

I said, "If you were my half brother, my dad would have told me."

Charlie said, "No, he wouldn't. You know how he hides everything."

I didn't believe him at all and left. I called my dad, and he didn't answer his phone, and the next day was the wedding.

The wedding was short. She wore a scalloped light-green dress. She was tiny and built nicely. The dress was weird, but she looked happy. I was seated at the family table as was Charlie and his fiancée. I spoke to my dad, danced with him, and he asked that I call her my stepmom.

I said, "*No.* I have a mom, and I don't need a step anything."

He got mad at me saying that I was ungrateful since he brought me there to enjoy his day.

I said, "I know you asked the boys too and friends of yours (all a shot in the dark as I didn't really know), and I am the only one that came. So you are lucky to have one person here just for you, but instead you make ridiculous demands. Also, why do you have those sleazy mirrors on your bedroom ceiling?"

He said, "We are done! You argue just like your mother and are mean sometimes."

"Dad, I am well. At least I don't hit women and get loud sloppy drunk, so I'll be happy with myself!"

I left the reception and changed into swimming gear and went swimming. I just wanted to be alone. But *no,* here comes Charlie. Charlie said that he was sorry that I was jealous of him being my father's son. That his mother was a nice kind person, and it would be nice if I could accept her as she always wanted a daughter.

I about flipped the fuck out. "She is not my mother, step, or whatever. I have a mother, and it is not yours. I still don't get you are my half-sibling anyway. I don't have to accept it if I don't want to anyway."

The next morning, I came out for breakfast and packed to leave a day early. I changed my ticket and was over it. I had enough. I got home to my apartment, where I lived alone at the time, and was happy to be home. I went out with some friends and said nothing to anyone about what I had experienced and caught up with Kathy afterward, and she said, "Just forget it."

How do you do that? I thought.

I can't and still haven't.

The next thing I found out was that they were going to Italy for their honeymoon. My mother had no idea I had gone to the wedding. Also, my mother and my aunt Terry had just made plans to go to, you guessed it, Italy. I didn't tell them they were going to be there at the same time, but I was so worried that they would run into each other because they'd frequent the same kind of places. Family secrets were so hard to keep, but I did it to keep the peace, or so I thought.

I also worked with a woman who knew my father's wife and son as well as this woman's mother. Debbie, who I worked with, had a mom who worked for my dad's wife's mom. She was her housemaid and carer. Debbie grew up helping out and still helped out until twenty-two years before, in other words when Charlie was born. This is when she said to me that Tim, my dad, Debbie knew. She knew that they told everyone the baby's father was a merchant seaman. I had heard that too, hence why I didn't believe Dad was his father. My mouth dropped and got it; he was probably my half brother, but I didn't have to accept him, especially since my dad hid him the whole time. Sad but true unless he told me it was okay to deny it. But Debbie hadn't worked for her or her mother for years now and worked with me at Donnelly Directory. A few weeks passed and nothing happened.

My parents didn't run into each other, and for that, I was grateful. But a few days later, I got a phone call from my dad, and he was crying to the point I couldn't understand him. She died. I found out from Dad she died like her own mother died—from a lung aneurysm—and he couldn't help her. They were getting ready to go on cruise to the Bahamas when she was in the kitchen and was unable to breath. Debbie explained to me that this is exactly how her mother died. Charlie, on the other hand, blamed my dad for not getting help on time. There was no time. She dropped dead, and there was no medical intervention nearby. He was blaming him for not getting her help on time, where he did try. The funeral was sad because there was no one there for Dad again, just like his wedding. However, his wife's best friend was there and was very caring toward Dad. Well, six months later, they were married too. He was married to her for twelve years until she died too. My mother is the only one that survived his marriages. During this time, my father's dementia got worse, from others letting my brother know. The family of his last wife blamed him for her death too. There was fear that they'd hurt him as they were rednecks that ran in trucks with long guns everywhere.

This was when I found out that my mother wanted to get him back to Pennsylvania because he was totally alone and possibly in danger. Dad's dementia was bad, and Mom went down to see him, thinking that he'd be different, had grown since their divorce. The dementia stole any hope of that, and his being bipolar didn't give her a chance with this man. She didn't want to remarry; she just wanted closure that was not so viscous as the divorce was. He asked her to marry him again, and when she said no, he became nasty and mean-spirited toward her, so she left. But she got him there to Pennsylvania anyway, but that was with my oldest brother's help. He paid for a great deal of my father's end of life care, and for that, I am heartily grateful. I never could have done what he did. This man was vile to Tim, yet he did the right thing with his abilities to do so. Not everyone would do that, not even would an ex-wife.

Chapter 7

Dad lived on his own at this point, and I lived in Scranton, Pennsylvania, over two hundred miles away with Nancy, my partner at the time.

I met her in 1990 and we ended in 1999. In 1998, Dad was still with us mentally to a degree, but it was clear he had dementia. Mom would go places with him. Susan, my sister-in-law through Tim, did a lot as well. She organized him and helped make sure he made appointments.

My relationship at the time with Nancy was a mess. It was broken from the start. I was looking to fix someone, and she was looking to own someone. I can see that now, but then, of course, I couldn't. Hence I began therapy. Nancy was seeing a person on her own. I, on the other hand, went to Jewish Family Services to find someone that didn't charge and ended up with a social worker who was my first counselor. The primary thing she had me do was the most damaging thing anyone could have done. She had me write letters to my abusers, which included my father. I started with Dad's, and I figured we'd talk about it in session. Instead I was supported to send it to my dad, and I said a lot in this letter. But Dad was at my brothers' for a visit, and when he got his letter, so did Tim. The next thing I knew, I had no family. My mother called me asking me what she was supposed to do about it and why I was trying to ruin our family. No one spoke to me for two years, and I missed out on my nephews growing up because of it. I knew that this wasn't right, but I became despondent and suicidal at this point. I was planning my own demise as it felt like it was the only way out of a situation that I had gotten myself into.

I ended up in Chestnut Hill Hospital for help because I had enough and just wanted this to stop. It was 1995. I was thirty-five and totally alone in my own head, very selfish with my thoughts and feelings. I was put on all kinds of medications and was diagnosed as dipolar. At this point, I had to find a therapist to help keep me in the right mind, and I did. I found a wonderful woman named Minna.

I worked with Minna for over seven years, and if it wasn't for that work, I wouldn't be here today. We connected in a way wherein I could see what it was like to have a parent who would actually care without fault and selfishness; nothing was predicated on what I did or didn't do. It lacked enmeshment and codependency like all my other relationships had always looked like. Yep, the work I did with her also helped me heal from the mistake of sending the letters to my family complaining about them, accusing them of all that was wrong with me. This still didn't help at first for me to leave the situation I was in with Nancy. I was afraid of her, of what she would do and had threatened. I had seen her follow through on her threats, so I was aware that it would come to pass, which in time she tried. But the work I had done was formidable, so I finally began to entertain the idea of leaving her and let the "chips fall where they may." I realized that I couldn't live like this anymore. It was better to take on her emotional, financial, and physical assaults versus living in fear of them. At least when they transpire, I could handle them one at a time. It's much harder to fight the thoughts of what will happen than to actually contend with them. In your head, they are insurmountable, but in reality, it is bad but doable, and you will find an ending to that situation. Then we kept working on a plan for me to leave, but I was scared. I tried so many times until it finally happened on Valentine's Day of 1999.

I had wanted to break up with her but couldn't with the grip she had on me. We had been through unsuccessful pregnancy attempts in New York and in Pennsylvania. We had a business that did well and was really just taking off, and I wanted to go back to university to get a degree in psychology. She frightened me into staying, telling me all she could do to ruin me. Then on her birthday of June 1999, Nancy was pissed about what I didn't do for her birthday. To be clear, she wanted balloons. So I went to get them, and on my way back, I was hit by an ambulance going over one hundred miles an hour while I was sitting still behind a stopped car. So I was hit twice—once by the ambulance and then shoved into and under the Pontiac in front of me—and I was in a fourteen-year-old Nova. Nancy acted like I was dying when she got to the hospital. The female police officer with me kept rolling her eyes, which made me wince in pain with laughing. I had severe whiplash injury, and years later, I still have issues with my back and advanced arthritis and fibromyalgia due to this accident.

But on the day of the accident, I was still in the hospital, and Nancy wanted me to get a lawyer and call my brother to do something. I had thought that I was sure this man didn't get up that day and was clearly thinking that he was going to do something stupid and hit me. Hence, why they call them accidents, not "on purposes," as my dad would say. She was royally angry with me about this, but I was just trying to heal. Wearing neck gear wasn't pleasant, and my back hurt like the dickens. But one day, in the mail comes a bill from the same ambulance company that hit me for picking me up from the accident and taking me to the hospital. I thought it was a mistake and called them. I said, "My insurance company paid what's to be paid, and your company is the reason I am in this condition in the first place." She agreed, or so she said. In the interim, my life changed drastically.

After the accident, I had a lot of time for soul searching. I finally decided to break up with someone I no longer loved, not even liked anymore. I felt sorry for her and said I'd stay and pay rent until I found a place and she figured things out on her end. No, that didn't work, and she became violent. I grabbed the wall phone in the kitchen to call the police.

I thought to myself, *Here we go, just like when I was a kid.*

Jezzuz, I was pissed at myself. She grabbed the handle, smashing my hand into the wall. In the meantime, the cops arrived and said it would be best that I leave for the night. I had a dog and no place to go, so my dog was left, which worried me, and I went to a hotel. But the police took me to an organization in the area for women in abusive situations. They were so wonderful and had to fight through my defenses for me to see that this was abuse. I was being emotionally, sexually, and financially abused by her. I kept saying no, but in time working with them and my therapist, I understood, and my mental health at this time was fragile. Then I went to a hotel, and I just started school at Marywood. This pissed her off too, so I finally got to realize that when she said I was too stupid to go to university, she was only saying what I believed. So I decided to go because I knew that the belief was from my childhood and not in the here and now. But she did all she could to interfere and put more negatives in my head daily. That is abusive.

I was beginning to grow and said that I realized at thirty-nine years old, I had been fifteen for twenty-four years and never moved forward. I was still that emancipated, institutionalized-type kid who knew how to survive but not how to live. I needed to figure that out, and what better way to do it than to move, live alone, and go to school. Challenge those ridiculous beliefs that weren't truly even mine. They were echoes of my childhood alive and well dancing in my head. I moved out into the school's old master's program facilities for free, and a number of nuns helped me hide my dog, "Girlfriend," from the mother superior. It was fun. The nuns had prayers at certain times of the day, and Girlfriend joined the festivities until she was done with it and would let them know. She was adored and cared for in a way that I was so blessed. She was blessed also. The Jewish community came through too and helped me get a place to finally live in, and I moved out into an apartment, hiding all the time from Nancy. She had broken down badly and was constantly looking for me and really did expect me to return. That would never happen as I was afraid of her and felt so sad for her. She didn't have to take this route. She even called my school and spoke to my superior and said a whole lot of slanderous stuff about me. But Sister Cabral came through with "we know you, and we know her." I was shocked that they knew her, but they did. I forgot that Scranton was really a very small town. You couldn't fart without someone's family member knowing.

Living in the apartment, I had to hide my car in the back and watch my back everywhere I went, including when I walked

Girlfriend or when I was on campus. Finally I had a place, people who were watching out for me, and I never once even got any help from my family. Not even an offer then, and it would have been nice to have that, but I didn't. So I had friends and those I would rather have as friends or chosen family.

Then about a month later, I got a warning letter which I ignored as just a mistake they made, and I didn't have time to sit on the phone for an hour. Then the red one came that they were suing me for the money. Then I found a lawyer. Tom was a graciously astute lawyer and was very kind. He also knew Nancy.

At this time, Nancy seemed to forget all that I had done for her, including running a business that she did nothing with or in. But she had her hand out. Instead she remembered the car accident and heard I was suing for $93,000, which I have no idea where she came with that and decided to sue me for that amount, trying to get my settlement if there was one.

This is when Tom said, "Remember I told you I know her?" And I was intrigued. He showed me a list of all lawsuits that she was involved with over the years, and they were like a Greek scroll. I was flabbergasted. I knew she sued her ex-partner and threatened her too but not much further than that. She sued companies, her family, anyone she could.

Tom asked me what I wanted to do first, and I said the most I will give her is half of the money spent on the attempts to have a baby, which was $25,000. Remember, this was the 1990s pricing.

He said, "You shouldn't give her anything, but we will abide by your request."

So finally there was a court date that I had to attend for her suing me. Tom was kind and asked that I bring my dad up, so he could feel part of the legal team. He let me know he knew who he was, but through me, he knew he was ill, and it was a mitzvah because he was a mensch that way. I actually asked that my mother and father to come to this situation in the court because I was scared, and I thought that they should. They did and I was shocked. The difference was I said what I meant and meant what I said, instead of hinting and hoping for it and more.

I was an adult with them for the first time. Dad was so excited that he was invited, but he was a royal pain in the butt. Dementia has its moments that are funny too, and I got to know the new man he was becoming, which was very sad. He did repeat himself a lot, and that was to be expected, and he did sundown early in the day but not so early that he couldn't go with us to the meetings and the actual court date. Tom said he heard that there was a problem with Nancy. She was searching around to find where I was staying and more. Tom put a PFA-type protection where she couldn't be within one hundred feet of me or my family. Also, she'd be in court for her portion and I for mine, but the two shall never meet. I was relieved, as was my mother. Dad was impressed and said so. He actually said, "You did well finding this attorney." I approve if that means anything. I called him a jerk, and we laughed. *Oh my god*, we laughed, and it was something I didn't think I'd experience with him *ever*.

I was actually deposed and that was all. Then we got an answer from the courts stating that they'd accept my offer, and that would happen if I win anything. That was to scare me and had my apartment ransacked, even with the dog there. I had enough. A friend from England invited me to go to her home and have a vacation from it all. So a friend took my dog, and I actually went abroad as I saw it as an opportunity to relax, and I liked this woman a lot even though she was married.

Chapter 8

Kaz was fourteen years my junior, and I knew it would never last, but it did last fourteen years of which we were actively involved for about eleven years. She had another woman she was involved with prior to my meeting her named Petra, and all the while she was married to Owen. Until I left, I can clearly state that for the entire twenty-plus years of marriage, she had a side girlfriend. A lot of that time was me. I believed in her and her strengths, even though there was a lot of depression and self-loathing. She had a larger-than-life personality to me. She was demanding, clear on her needs and how to meet them, and yet made it look like she was innocent of anything that she did or said. Yes, another narcissist.

When I first met her, her son was three years old and was a handful so much that Kaz had black eyes from his temper tantrums. The truth was he was undiagnosed with Asperger's or high-functioning autistic. Kaz didn't work due to her depression and agoraphobia. She could only go out with someone with her. She too is a survivor of childhood trauma.

Owen, her husband, and Ryan's father had undiagnosed Asperger's too, who by the way is a lovely man. However, she had me believe that her son was born out of his raping her. It took me a little while to realize that she was lying to me to keep me on the hook, waiting for her to break from being in that marriage. Again, I believed her and learned to believe what I wanted and knew when she was lying and still waited for her to break up with her husband. With all that said, I didn't have to completely commit to a relationship with her because I did help a lot with their son. Owen, at the beginning of our relationship, wasn't home during the week. He was only home on the weekends. Karen and I had friends that knew we were seeing each other as more than friends. Sara, Sharon, and more but they never broke the confidence. They didn't know Owen at first either as he was never home, so I guess it didn't seem odd until he came back to work from home.

At this time, I had been going to school in the USA at Marywood. She knew I was waiting for the lawsuit to settle, which took another seven years. They both helped me live there in the UK as I initially was there as a visitor, but I found that Marywood was a bit too easy, so I checked out the schools in the UK. I got accepted at the University of Essex's psychology program. They accepted my previous school grades, and I worked hard to get my BS in psychology from this school. I did it, I finished something I started, and I finished well. I may have done this at a school overseas, but it was what taught me how to learn even better than any other education I had before.

I helped around the house at home with the child and the house and dogs, even fed them, including the husband. Things were going swimmingly wherein Owen wasn't home that much, and we had a relationship that worked. Their son's behaviors were sincerely problematic because society didn't understand this great kid. He was smart, funny, adorable but lacking social skills. At this point, Owen decided to work from home for then on. He decided to run his own business and work for others as a project manager for computer companies. Owen's coming home permanently was the slow end of the relationship for me. See, she didn't sleep with her husband. She slept with me downstairs in the lounge in a couch bed that we'd open every night. Then she made it so that we slept head to toe, not next to each other upright. She said that it made him think nothing was happening. There was no way that I'd believe that bullshit now, but I did then.

This situation continued after I finished my BA as I decided to get my master of science in psychology too. I had finally realized I could finish something and complete the first degree; now I wanted to gain a degree of a higher award. And this meant that I'd have to stay and continue living this way and hope to see our relationship finally come to fruition, more than an affair.

I attended Anglia Ruskin University in Chelmsford and trained at Basidlon Hospital with the infamous Dr. Dianne Lefvere, and it was amazing. Extremely difficult but only three of us completed it to the masters of science degree in "severe personality and thought disorders." During that time, I realized how much help I must have to continue with supervisory therapy and private therapy so I could finish. Then I couldn't walk anymore. I was dragging my legs so badly that I ended up in a wheelchair for three years to go anywhere. In two years, while working on my MSc degree, I had both my knees replaced. However, I continued to have training hours in the UK at the hospital before and after I finished my degree. By the time I was forty-four years old, I had my bachelor's and my master's degrees and two new knees, and my dad passed away in the interim.

That took me by surprise. Not his death but my response. At first I didn't even seem to feel a loss, then one day, out of seemingly nowhere, I broke down and cried for days. I wasn't crying over the loss of who he was. I was broken over the fact that nothing would ever have a chance to change anymore. The relationship was broken, and I was mourning the loss of the relationship we could have had; my fantasy father was dead too. Dad found out I got my degrees and asked me why I would do that when I was "so old" to be going for degrees. That was his loving way of showing how jealous he was of his kids. Mom didn't come to my graduations of which she was requested to come to both. The family I lived with did, but that was crappy in my opinion. Yet I realized then that it may have taken me five years to do my masters with a dissertation, but I wasn't stupid. I was more than capable. I had to prove to myself that all the perniciousness of my childhood to adulthood chronic abuse didn't stop me. It may have delayed me a bit, but I got there in the end. I did it.

Then I won my case from the lawsuit against the ambulance company nine years later. That money was gone in no time. I brought my narcissist mother and her sister over to visit. But I couldn't let them stay with us as the house was absolutely a mess at all times. The carpets were frayed and falling apart, and the fact that there were three fully functional adults and a teen along with four dogs living in the equivalent of a starter home in the US. But it's what I had to live with—people I knew how to trust and with what. Yet it was a house of extreme secrets like I've explained.

My aunt and mother stayed at a bed and breakfast place nearby, and we had a great time, yet I felt I had to keep my aunt under my thumb with her acting out at times. Like one trip… We were going to see the castle at Dover and then the Secret Nuclear Bunker, and she'd say things like "Aaah, you seen one map room, you've seen them all." This family I lived with were breaking their time up to take them around and show them their country, and she was looking for the foods you'd eat at home. Well, she got it clear from me because I actually sent them to Scotland for a week to give us all a break. Mom and my aunt stayed a month in total, so one week was helpful for us and for them. I tried to please the ladies—Mom and Aunt Jane—and the family I lived with too, and there was no way to do that without falling on my face. What I wanted to do was a nice thing for my mother as she was in her eighties and had a long trip to her favorite country besides the US, which of course was the UK. She was appreciative and did have a good time. There were moments of absolute joy when she was there too. We played Uno one night for hours and drank beer and laughed till our hearts' content. The anxiety I had trying to please everyone was intense to the point that I needed help with my therapist and medication. It was harder than doing my dissertation for my master's degree.

This memory helps me know I was a good daughter. Even though I wasn't perfect, I did my best, and that's all I could do. Having my mother and Kaz there together was like a real headbanger because what I saw was I was involved with a woman who was very much like my mother. They even commented on how alike they were in their ways. Narcissistic love, I guess. A month felt like a year, and when they went home, I heard about all that was wrong of course. I began to separate from Kaz as time was approaching the destruction of the relationship that I could actually see and was experiencing. We still slept together but did not have sex anymore. That died, and I didn't know how to approach Kaz anymore about her decisions as to whether she was going to break from Owen or not. She'd say, "I told you I have to wait until I can break away financially from him, or you take care of me and Ryan. I mean, you can't afford to do that!" Even though I did pay my way and a lot of the money I got from my lawsuit went into the house outside of my mom's trip, I went quiet and decided I needed to find a way to get back to the USA, which was with little money.

I took a trip home to the USA and met with my mother, telling her what I was doing. I didn't want to have to go back, but I had to. I had so much to either pack or sell. The cost of bringing fourteen years' worth of life was incredible, so I sold clothing by the pound and got about $1500 in the clothing and also from items like movies, DVD/CDs, and more. Kaz didn't ask me anything and didn't seem to be upset about how much I wasn't home or was selling all my stuff. Then I bought a ticket home, which was cheaper to buy two ways over a one way ticket. I finally gave her the date I was leaving, which was November 4, 2015, for good. She was shocked and really didn't believe me. I guess after fourteen and a half years of making threats that I'd leave gave her that impression. Just like Nancy's thinking that I may have left but I would come crawling back. When I finally realized what I had done and wasted fifteen years with Kaz and ten years with Nancy, it was time to find the right life, the one that would be accepted by my family. The woman who would see me as important and as important as I would see her to be in my life. Love was expected, but I found that I was always attracted to those who were no good for me.

I actually was able to accept a position at a job near my mother and brother before I even left the country to come home. I knew then I had decided correctly. I moved in with my eighty-eight-year-old mother thinking I could help her for a bit and that it would be a place for me to land without demands. Oh my god was I wrong.

Chapter 9

At first I stayed there and worked full time. I worked long ridiculous hours with children and their families for their issues. Many were on the spectrum, and others had serious mental conditions. But the families were so broken, and I loved the work to help and support, creating treatment plans and more.

After a full day of work, which could be as long as twelve hours some days, Mom wanted to "do something," take her somewhere, or hang out at least. I wanted to hide and relax. It took me a few months to realize that my mother and I fell right into the enmeshed historical relationship we always had. I was so angry with myself and wanted to meet someone finally. I thought to myself, *How am I going to get away from her when I want to start dating at the age of fifty-five?* See, Mom divorced at fifty-three and never dated anyone ever again. She stayed single but had a load of friends. She seemed happy, but I wasn't willing to shut down just because I sucked at picking partners. I mean, I picked one that was already married; now that's bad. At fifty-five years old, where do you look? I was not going to the clubs anymore, and what and where are people looking too? Yep, you guessed it, I used a dating app site called Plenty of Fish, which took a while.

Why did it take so long? Because there are really horny older folks that want no relationships, just sexual ones. I wasn't looking for that as I had been through that. I thought that I was too old, too fat, just too much. That and when you state you're a counselor or a therapist, people run the other way. Maybe not physically but often they'll either want you to help them diagnose a friend, or they shut down thinking you know what they are thinking before they even think it!

One woman spoke to me online for a few weeks and was the head of a care home in Pennsylvania. She was interesting, age was in line, but she kept asking me when we were going to meet to have sex. That just pushed me the other way that I stopped talking to her. I started to feel like this was way too pushy or a male acting as a female. So I asked for a phone call to chat at first, and when that was denied, I stopped talking to them. Then there were people I knew. I mean, knew from high school. *No way*, thank you. Then there were those that wanted you to take care of them, and they were in their thirties and forties with kids. Having already been through that life, I wasn't going to do it again. I remember thinking it took me over forty years to think of myself first in a relationship and not what I could do for them—fix them, make it better, or help.

I spoke to so many and met with one, just one. We talked for a while on the phone, and she lived an hour away. She offered to come my way, yet I did explain I lived with my mother, which I thought would scare the daylights out of her. She said she questioned it, but she too was still living with her ex-partner of twenty-two years when we were just beginning to talk, so she thought who was she to judge. She drove over an hour to meet me at a Starbucks. She didn't realize I had only been back in the USA for a few months and hadn't ever lived in the area we were meeting, in West Chester, Pennsylvania.

I met her and saw the most piercing beautiful blue eyes and a kind demeanor with a quiet type of personality. She is eight years my junior, which unnerved me thinking that I was too old for her. But instead she stayed and drank coffee with me. The longer we talked, the more anxious I got because I immediately liked her and felt nervous. An hour in and I used the excuse that I had to help my mother with her dinner; that just wasn't true at that time. What was true was my stomach was one big butterfly, and I knew I had met "the one" and never experienced that before. I felt so unnerved that I had to leave and regroup. Poor thing said she didn't realize that and just didn't get why she had driven an hour to see me to meet for less than an hour. But we talked immediately and made another date to meet for dinner. I was lucky she didn't think she had just met a mommy's little girl at fifty-five years old. She gave me a chance, and we met for a lovely dinner and chatted about so much. I can't recall the topics, but it was like we were trying to get to know each other as quickly as possible, and in the middle of the meal, I broke a tooth. I was too shy to tell her that.

It was at about 8:00 p.m., and I said that I needed to get my mother to bed because I was embarrassed. Here I was, out for a meal at fifty-five, and I was falling apart as I spent an hour with her. Then I made arrangements to go to her house instead of her coming to me. I parked in the flower-edged rounded driveway and up close in the back of the house. What a beautiful house with a koi pond in the back, and her dog was barking his fool head off. This was my first experience of meeting a pit bull, so I was, let say, *terrified* but pushed through. I was *not* leaving this woman again and going to have a full date, where we could get to talk and speak to each other. I also planned to stay over. Her ex was staying at her new girlfriend's house, and we could finally get to be alone in a private setting. *Nice*, in my opinion.

I walked up five steps while she held Tbone by his collar to keep him calm. I walked up and he bit my handbag. I ran to a chair and sat down. I let him sniff me and come to me. I scratched his little, tiny butt, and he and I were almost immediately friends.

I thought, *Good. One down and the main one is next, Tara.*

I brought food and thought that I would show off my ability as a cook. I made a very basic meal of roasted chicken, mashed potatoes, gravy, and salad. We both ate well and laughed a lot through the meal at Tbone's reaction to me by biting my hand ag. We had to use a blowup bed that night since the other bed had been used by her ex and her girlfriend over the years, and we didn't want that.

Then every time Tara and I got close, Tbone would bark and say what he felt, whereas the other dog who belonged to the ex, Onyx, was a Labrador who would take all things on the floor to her kennel, which at this point in time I didn't know where. I set down my iced tea in a bottle and left the room for a minute to check on dinner. I thought this was weird, and yep, my bottle of iced tea was in her kennel. Too blinking cute and I fell in love with her ex's dog too. I wanted to steal her, to be honest, because at this time, it had been almost a year since I didn't have a dog. I had been with a dog since I was five years old and felt like without one, I was missing a part of myself.

We started to date, and we did so exclusively for a year. But that Christmas, I knew she was the one, so I asked her to marry me, and she said yes. Here I am at fifty-five with all the crap I had to live through, all the chronic trauma, and Tara still showed how she loved me by allowing me to be myself and I to her. We didn't interfere with each other's life choices, but we did try to meet each other's families as they are blood. It went well until the wedding when Tara's brother wouldn't come because he was a homophobic religious zealot. The wedding was small and pushed up about six months because at forty-five, getting into the presidency we weren't sure we could marry when we wanted to, which was in the summer. We married on December 10, 2016. Mom came wrapped in her long mink coat that dwarfed her, but she wasn't going to the wedding without it. We got married in a small ceremony at a friend's *farmette* that was beautiful and by the fireside. My entire family came to the wedding, and the friends and those like family for Tara came and also mutual friends, but it was an awesome druid-type wedding. We were both giggly and goofy about the fact that we could call each other wife and how funny that sounded. We also didn't think that the marriage part would make a big difference with our relationship. We couldn't be more wrong. I never felt so supported in a relationship. Knowing that, being married helped us know we made promises in front of those we respected and trusted that we'd work on our relationship as it continues after we wed.

We are both survivors of chronic lifetime traumas that many would fold under and have done so. I wrote this for seven years and was six years married to say that one can make it through and find that one or few who can make you have a life that is no longer crisis driven and from a chronic traumatic time. It is something that we can respect our histories but not live them as we age. We have to know sometimes we make mistakes, we fall back into old ways, but that's not to say you cannot change them each time that transpires. Moving forward and onward is a process that is serially imperfect. Just like in anyone's life, we make mistakes. Those are all surmountable as long as we work on ourselves throughout our lifetime. Life is nothing more than a process of processes. What we learn is up to us.

About the Author

Jeanne Callahan is a retired counselor who is happily living the life of a retiree. She has a wife of seven years and a canine crew of four dogs. She loves to write and the obligatory desire to garden. Life was tough, and now she is experiencing a great part of her life. The past is to be celebrated, not wallowed.